GRACE

JILL PATON WALSH

Grace

Farrar Straus Giroux
New York

*To the memory of 'a good girl,
about whom a great deal of nonsense was talked'*

Text copyright © 1991 by Jill Paton Walsh
Map copyright © 1991 by Hanni Bailey
All rights reserved
Library of Congress catalog card number: 91-31054
First published in 1991
by Viking Kestrel / Penguin Books Ltd, London
Printed in the United States of America
First American edition, 1992
Third printing, 1994

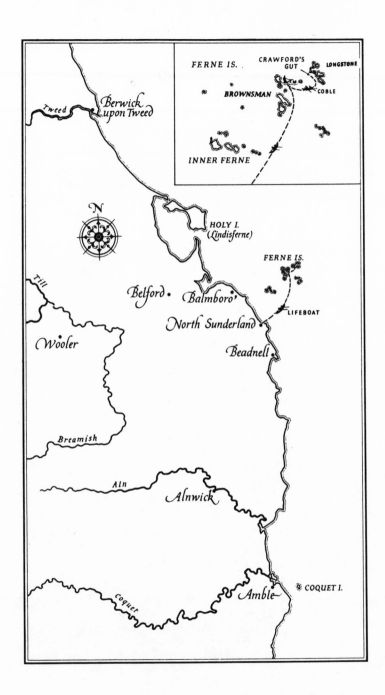

FERNE IS.

CRAWFORD'S GUT

LONGSTONE

BROWNSMAN

COBLE

INNER FERNE

Tweed

Berwick upon Tweed

N

HOLY I. (Lindisferne)

FERNE IS.

Belford

Bamboro'

North Sunderland

LIFEBOAT

Till

Wooler

Beadnell

Breamish

Aln

Alnwick

Coquet

Amble

COQUET I.

· 1 ·

We had been up in the night. Father reckoned it the highest tide we had known since we lived on the Longstone Rock, and a fierce storm was blowing. We had to leave our beds, and go forth into the wrath of the weather, to bring the chattels within the shelter of the outhouse walls, and lash down the coble which is our only boat, binding it upside down. The water would be certain to surge and smash over the rocks to the foot of the lighthouse tower, and higher, and soon would be into the kitchen, but if all was made secure our losses would be small. We were wet to the skin in the blast and the weight of flying water the moment we stepped out, and we had a struggle to do what we needed. It would have been better, much better, had my brother Brooks been with us, but he was on the mainland, that night, in North Sunderland, and not to be expected in the morning, in the prospect of such weather ahead.

When we got in again I took off my shawl and my dress, and put them on the rail before the warm stove, to dry, along with Father's jacket and trousers. But my shift and my stockings I wore wet and clinging till I reached my bedside, and there took

7

them off and spread them on the back of a chair, and took a dry shift from the cupboard. I was ready enough to return to the fading warmth between my bed-sheets. My room is the last below the lantern floor, and eighty feet above the Longstone rocks, but the water was leaping between me and the moonlight, and knocking hard against my curving windows. I could hear nothing in the roar of it, not a creak nor a clicking of the lamp engines over my head that is commonly my lullaby. But I am certain the lamp was shining, for the shadow of the lantern platform moves across my window, and I fell asleep seeing it. It was in my mind to watch for it in the moments before I slept; a poor bird with such a force behind it, as has happened before, might strike clean through the glass, and let the winds snuff the lamp.

Father woke me at four, when my watch begins, and went to his bed. I rose, and dressed, and having checked the lamps and their oil, I returned to my room, and sat upon a chair to watch for first light. We must be thrifty with lamp-oil, and quench the burners as soon as they are overtaken by day. I did not look out of my window before climbing the stair again, for the exhalation from my clothing had thickly beaded and dewed the cold windows, and made them unclear.

But when I was aloft I looked towards the Brownsman Island, which once was home to me, where we used to be above the reach of the ocean in the kitchen, and where a few flowers grew, and creatures crept to keep us company, and where we still have a

8

garden, walled round with stones from the abandoned buildings, ours when we can reach it. Every morning I look in that direction first, and see our little cottage, and the stump of the abandoned former light tower. And there, between me and the expected sight, looming up, was a frightful and pitiful thing – the frontmost part of a great ship, struck on the rock we call Big Harker, and with the water clawing and going over her, and most of her top gear taken off by wind or wave.

In the murk of the lowering dawn, through curtains of rain and spray it showed faintly, like a vessel of ghost or dream, and for one moment I thought I was still sleeping, and dreaming the drift of the book I had been reading when I went to my bed last night, which was a sermon of Bishop Collison, about the shipwreck of souls.

Then I cried out, and I clambered down the stairs – we must go backwards on the spirals – through my bedchamber to my father and mother's room below, shouting on my father all the way. 'A wreck, Father! A wreck!' I was calling, and he, drawing on his trews as he answered, said, 'Now God help us, and Brooks away!'

He ran up the stairs towards me, holding his unfastened trousers with one hand, and buttoning his shirt with the other. So I regained the lantern with my father at my back, and together we looked out.

The worst of the storm's force had abated, and yet there was a mighty wind still blowing, and a great swell breaking over both wreck and rock together. And it was barely light, being then one quarter before five. My father gazed through the telescope which he kept always on a stand in the lantern, while I looked through his field-glasses; we stood incessantly scanning the scene, standing side by side in the stench of the quenched wicks, and the carbon black from the uncleaned reflecting mirrors, and the slowly fading odour of the cooling lamp-oil. The dawn was slow and sullen, bringing on but a murky light, and the wind and the salt-spatter against the windows obscured our view.

My father went out upon the lantern platform but could not hold the telescope steady in the gale. My mother brought coffee to the foot of the stair, and I ran down for it. And all this while we saw not a sign of movement, other than the fury of the water. Slowly, though, we made out the rake of the tilting deck, and a great wheel, almost on top of it, so steeply did she slope in her disaster.

'What is she, Father?' I asked him.

'A steam vessel, of such a size?' he said. 'I think it is the *Forfarshire*, though God grant it be some other . . .'

'Why, Father?' I asked him, my heart cold.

'Because her freight is of men,' he said. 'She is a passenger ship.'

'How many souls, Father, do you guess?'

'It cannot have been below fifty,' he said. 'Keep scanning, girl.'

Then we were very quiet, he as much as me, I imagine, weighed down by such a sight of doom. But just before seven the storm tore a hole in the black sky, and let a brief gleam of brightness through, and with that I thought I saw movement, and it was not upon the vessel, but on the rock itself. My father at my direction swung the spy-glass to play upon the rock, where it sloped steeply and gave a little lee; and he had no doubt of seeing some poor creatures clinging there. He could not count them, though we reckoned them upwards of five.

Somehow they must have got themselves upon the rock for safety, that could not have known what scant safety it offered them. For our reef of islands divides the tides, so that there is a double movement to them; and already the second surges threatened what foothold they had.

We racketed down the stairs, and flung back the bolts of the door, and into the cold scour of the open air, to look at a man's view of the matter, rather than the bird's view of the lantern floor.

'Can we get them? Can it be done, Father?' I asked.

'If Brooks were here it might,' he said.

Well we knew it took three men to handle our coble in rough water, though I have hundreds of times been one of two to take her oars in calm. 'I must take Brooks's part,' I said.

'Give over, and come indoors,' my mother said, coming out behind us. 'This is not for us. The castle guns have fired, and the lifeboat will come out.'

'I doubt it,' Father said. 'The waves will be over the breakwater at North Sunderland, and into the harbour. They have five miles to pull with the gale against them all the way. And this is the storm's eye, not the storm over. Look at the weather.' And indeed there was the foulest sky looming that ever I saw, and the mainland not in sight in the daylight blackness. But over our heads was a grey light fingering through a thinness in the ugly sky, and the swell at our feet was sullen, flint-black, not breaking white.

We withdrew, into the kitchen. 'But someone *must* help them!' I said.

'Harken, Grace,' my father said. 'We cannot go straight there, close though it be. We would be blown sideways on to the rocks without let. But perhaps we might go the long way; we might let the coble drive before the wind till it gets south of the reef, and then row in the lee . . . the wind would then be behind us, and the tide slackening for the turn as we are getting there, and you taking Brooks's oar . . . But for getting back we cannot do it unless one of those out there is strong enough to help us, for the wind and tide will be running hard against us on the return. If we get there, and we cannot get back, there will be no help for us. Will you take the risk?'

'Or otherwise we stand and watch them die?' I said. 'I would try it alone, if I had to.'

But he had known my answer, for as he spoke he was putting on his boots.

My spirit was so worked up by so dreadful an affair that I would have done anything, so that I might do something, and not stand helplessly watching. To unlash the coble and get it into the water was itself no small thing, and my mother had to help us, though all the while she set up a wailing and lament at our folly.

'Whist, woman,' Father said. 'Think of the premiums. That will stiffen thy courage.'

I ran upstairs, and tied my shawl about me, over my dress, and took up the blanket from my bed, in case it would succour someone, and my petticoat I discarded, for it is troublesome to get the flannel of it dry from such a wetting. This took me but a short time; I did not stop to take the curl-papers from my hair, but pulled a bonnet on over.

And when the coble was turned rightways up, and set into the water, bucking like a frightened horse, and my mother held on to it while I got in before Father, she said to me, 'Oh Grace, if your faither is lost, I'll blame aa' you for this morning's work!'

'Strike!' cried Father, and we pulled away.

That it was a hard service none would doubt me who knew the waters that we needed to cross. And the worst of it was the first of it, for we had to pass through the gap we call Crawford's Gut, that divides the Longstone from the Blue Caps and the Harker Rocks, and the waters came furiously raging through there, chopped into buffeting fury by the unbroken wind.

I thought my oar would snap, or be torn out of my hand, and no better than one heave in three held in the grip of water. Lurching, we pulled on the light spume and the empty air, as the boat tipped and tossed, and righted ourselves how best we could. And when the oars found purchase the choppy water levered them allgates about, battering and bruising us, and giving us a forward thrust with them little enough to make me fear we would spend all our strength in the fury of Crawford's Gut, and never go more than fifty yards towards our aim. My father is a strong man, but he could not his hardest; for if he pulled harder than I, the coble's head turned and we lost direction. And the wind whipped and lashed into our faces, as we rowed before it, so that I was blinded all the way.

Then at last we drew under the shelter of the Blue Caps, and were rowing in the lee of the rocks, while the wind tore over above us. Just below the rocks the water was smoother, the surface like shards of flint, troubled but not broken, so that we felt the wisdom of my father's decision to come the long way round the skerries. We rowed with something less of difficulty then, till I glanced over my shoulder, and saw quite near us the great bulk of the looming ship, and the folk on the rock all screaming and wailing and crowding to the edge of the water, to see us coming.

They scared me more than the storm did. I thought in their terror they would seize us and swamp us. Nine of them. And they looked like devils, distraught.

'Keep her steady, if you can, Grace,' said Father, and in the last instant before any of the crazed grasping hands could reach us, he jumped from the cross-thwart, and I was alone in the rocking coble, and he on the rock.

I heard not a word of the conferring that went on only a yard or two to the side of me; the wind whipped words away, and all I could see was that

Father was shouting to be heard, and others shouting in answer.

It was as much as I could manage to keep the coble steady, and near the rock. I had need of both oars to do it, and a coble is a little wide for such a way of rowing. I contrived it, and from the corner of my eye as I struggled I saw the distress of the only woman on the rock. They were dragging her two children from her clasp, while she howled – all in dumb show, for I could hear nothing but the roar of wind and water – and resisted. Only as she lost her hold, from the way the children slumped and dangled in the arms of the seamen did I understand that they were both dead, and she perhaps did not.

It was only a few short minutes that I contended alone in the boat on which our eleven lives all depended; then Father seized the thwart, and swung himself on board again. And we had reckoned rightly, God be thanked for it, that there would be seamen, strong and sensible men, among the survivors, for now the woman was lifted across the thwarts, and laid sitting slumped against the side, forward, and an injured man was lifted in and laid likewise aft, and Father put blankets over them, though the blankets were sodden enough. Then three strangers climbed aboard the coble, so that she bore down deeper in the water. I sat on the midships, and in front of me rowed Father and another, and behind me two more, and so with four oars and still with no rudder shipped, and leaving four behind us till we came again, we pulled away. We had a mile to recover; and on a falling tide in the lee of the reef it was nothing fearful, till the last quarter mile, when turning into Crawford's Gut we had no shelter, and had to pull against wind and tide together. So we got her in again to the Longstone haven – a tiny sheltered crevice in our rocks, our only harbourage – and Father stayed but to help carry the woman and the sick man up the steps to the door, and lay them within.

'One to stay and two to go again,' he said. And there went with him one who turned from the sheltering door without hesitating – it was Mr Tulloch, I knew later – and one who hesitated only a second, looking back. And the third, seeing himself excused from duty, stooped to help raise the woman from the salt-washed floor, and assist her into the houseplace.

My mother was within, her sleeves rolled up, putting bellows to the fire below a pan of water. She turned on me a look of so blending relief and fear as I shall never forget it, and I said, before she could ask me, 'He is gone back. But there are two strong fellows with him.'

'He has gone to fetch me my babes again,' said the woman.

'Alas no,' I said to my mother. 'The poor bairns are dead with cold. He has gone for four others living, and there is one lying at the door now in a poor way.' The warmth of the kitchen had begun to gnaw cruelly at my frozen fingers and feet, and my teeth rattled together in my head.

'Go get dry clothes on, Grace, and come again to help me,' my mother said. And as I went, ascending the stair against the drag of the water in my heavy clothes, she passed me a billy-can of hot black tea.

It was the greater part of another hour, I think, while my father went and came again. In that time we had contrived to get Mrs Dawson up the stairs, and put to bed in my bed – for what other could we offer her? – and we had lifted the injured man in from beside the door and laid him on a pallet on the floor of the houseplace, beside the fire, and given him gruel in three small sips. We had mended the fire and coaxed it into a blaze with the bellows, and we had stripped off the ragged ribbons of clothes upon the uninjured man, poor fellow, in a stun, and hardly knew what befell him, and wrapped him in a dry blanket; and all the while we were whipped by anxiety, and flying about our errands as though Father's safety depended on it, as though should we pause to draw breath, or stand to tremble but a moment, he might founder. This while the storm was worsening again. Storms will do so; as a child will cry itself into silence, and then revive and greet again, so a storm will sulk a while, and then revive its fury. We could hear in our fear the buffeting winds, and the rage of the water.

But Father did not founder; he came again with the two who had turned back from the door to help him, and the four they had gone back for – seven men staggering in to us, their limbs leaden with weariness, and thick-witted with the night-long endurance of the cold. The confusion we were in was dreadful, then. With difficulty we got clothes sodden and sticky with salt off the men's backs, and out of the steaming kitchen, and got dry garments on to limbs stiff with cold and injury; found somewhere for so many to sit – we brought in oil barrels from the store, and set them as near the fire as we might; and the urgency of hot food kept Mother and me chopping bacon and potatoes and scooping lentils from the store into the pot. When Father first came in he went to my mother, and put a hand upon her shoulder, and said to her, 'See then?'

'What if it had gone worse, William?' she said, and then, 'Ah, but I cannot scold thee!'

At first the throng of folk in our small room brought in the cold and wet, and we were all shivering and discomfortable; but soon the blazing fire defeated the cold, and drove the damp out on to the window-panes, where it mizzled like rain. The poor strangers began to fall sleeping where they sat. My father's chair was taken by another, so he sat on a barrel by the door, with a mortal weariness upon him. As I passed him going to the store he looked up at me.

'Well, Grace?' he said.

'Well, Father,' I answered him. I smiled a little as I gave again his simple word; for we had not at that moment the least apprehension but that we had done well.

· 2 ·

My mother has told me how the coble was scarcely in the water but she lost sight of us – the storm carried us over a mountain of rising water, and we vanished. She cried out, but could not catch the sound of her own voice in such an uproar. Then she ran in, and looked from the kitchen window, which is somewhat higher, and still could not see us. While she stared a great wave struck hard upon the glass, and held there, so that it seemed to her she was deep drowned herself, among all her kitchen tackle as she stood. This time she heard her own wailing, for she was shrieking like a ghost unto herself. She went higher then; scrambling into her bedchamber, and staring from the windows, lashed with spray, and she could yet catch no sight of us. So then she stood, her skirt dripping round her on the floor, and her limbs like lead. She told me – but little by little, for she is a woman of few words, and we were throng enough for many days after – how then in her misery she climbed the tower, all the way to the light.

I know not how to say with what amazement I heard her tell this. But we have been now twelve years upon the Longstone Rock, our masters, the masters of all lighthouses, the Brethren of Trinity House, having moved us from the Brownsman on February 15th, The Year of Our Lord 1826. That was an island; this a mere rock, washed over by any unusual tide. The move was at my father's urging; he putting the safety of seamen above his own comfort, or ours. But in that twelve-year time I have not known my mother climb any higher in the tower than her bedroom. I would say she has a fear of heights, in the way some people have that is near to a sickness. And what a thing it is, to be unwilling to climb in a place of such close confinement as our tower, where the weather may keep us many days together from any refreshing movement, any release of our powers, other than running errands up and down the stair.

So you can see how amazed I might be that Mother should have climbed into the lantern in her fright for us. She climbed up, and she could not see us. She saw the great ocean running in waves half as high as the tower, and not a sight of the coble. All round her the massy glasses and reflectors of the lantern glowered in the black storm-light like quenched coals, and below she saw the heaving water buck and sink, so that her eye could find no level and it seemed the tower itself was swaying and keeling over, and still no sight of the boat. She fainted then. And came to lying upon the floor, she could not tell how much later. She was puzzled at first, finding herself staring at the shining glasses above her; she wondered why her head was wedged against the wall. Then her terror returned to her, she knew herself deserted and alone for however many days it took for the storm to abate, and Brooks to reach the Longstone from the main; and she alone to keep the lights burning, as had never had any doing with them before. In terror she drew herself upon her knees, and heaving on the rail below the curving window she hauled herself standing, somehow, and as she did, she saw for a scrap of a moment the coble thrown up to the crest of a towering wave, and Father at his oar, and me at mine, and then we were gone again, vanished into the pit between one wave and another. But oh, she said, to know us still to be living!

She sank to her knees, then, and crawled to the stair, and weeping with relief and with fear together, descended, and began to mend the fire, and seek out dry clothes and bedding, as though she could be certain to be in need of them. She will tell anyone who will listen how long she was busied thus; the measure of dry split peas she had put into a pot on the fire for soup was cooked soft and ready before we came again, but come we did, and gladly did she set to scold us – me for the most part, for she is somewhat in awe of Father – for giving her so great a fright.

There is no gainsaying it – we had given my mother a bad time. My sister Thomasin is forever saying she would rather far have been in my place than in my mother's that morning. It does not cross her mind that my part was anything out of the common run; something she might not have done herself. I tell her, 'It would have blistered your fingers, Thomasin; you would not have held a needle for weeks!' She is a dressmaker. And now she is upon the mainland, and no longer living off, with the family and the sea-birds, her heart is torn, it seems to me. She would always like to think herself capable in any need, yet she would not like to think her absence could put us in any difficulty, for behind that thought comes closely a threat to her freedom, the shade of a need for her to return. This fear is in her mind rather than in others'; as long as I can remember, I have been the one expected to remain in my father's household, and share the burdens of my parents' life. I no longer know whether my father's eagerness to put books into my hands arises because he would have me fortified against solitude, or whether it is my inclination to book-reading that made him settle upon me in the first place. My sister would rather far be on the land, however. She has a hare-shed lip that makes her little likely to marry, and a skill with a needle that gives her no need of it; she can keep herself well enough. It was not Thomasin's being from home, but Brooks's flighting off to the mainland that put us in difficulties; things would have been different for us all had Brooks been at home that morning.

But nowadays Brooks is often on the main. My mother is much older than my father, and when Brooks and George were born she was already forty-five. She could not run about the low-tide rocks, keeping double-chucker boys from falling in. Almost as soon as I could walk I was looking to the boys, and minding them. I would have said in their growing days Brooks was like my father – a handy child, quick at learning any practical thing. He could splice ropes, and help Father with his model-making, and catch fishes, running lines from the rocks. He could spot the kinds of ship that passed us, and keep the outlookers' log in which the Brethren wished us to enter every vessel that we saw. He could climb for gulls' eggs on the stacks of Staples Island, and shoot eider duck and rabbits on the Brownsman, and fish for codling and herring from the rocks – a great fellow for a full larder! – and row the coble nimbly in the racing tides. He did not share my father's love of book learning, nor his liking for the naturalists, the gentlemen scholars who visited us, and corresponded with Father, though he had been at school in Balmboro', at the castle, which I envied him. Brooks like Father; George like Thomasin, always pining for the main. Father had set George on as an apprentice carpenter at Newcastle; but George once gone from us, Brooks felt the lack of a brother keenly. No sister would stand in stead for George; Brooks worked his share as before, but sullenly, and looked all the while for any chance to go rollicking with his bullies in Sunderland, helping with nets, and keeking pretty lasses, and drinking in the Ship, which Father called the beggar-maker's shop.

'I always thought him so like thee, Father,' I said once.

'Aye, Grace, aye,' Father said, smiling at me, 'every dog has his day.' He never rebuked Brooks those days. 'I too was brought up offshore, under my father's eye. I can well remember,' he said to me, 'how close a lighthouse felt to a sprightly youth; and that was the Brownsman, mind, not the Longstone, where it needs low tide to so much as unkink our knees and walk a yard.'

When I did not answer him, he said, 'Ye cannot picture me ganging on like Brooks, Gracie? How think ye your mother was won?'

'It's rather how Father was won!' said Thomasin, when I told her of this conversation. 'Why, Gracie, think you did Father wed with a gardener's daughter twelve year older than he? And she in the protection of the Crewe Trustees, thereafter to keep beady eyes on all that he did? He liking his own mastership as he does?'

'Fie, Thomasin!' I said to her. 'For sure, it was love . . .'

'He was lodging under the same roof as she, and love takes many forms,' said Thomasin. I take no note of the half that she says; she has a sharp tongue, and she bridles under Father's governance, which irks not me.

So there have been, in all, nine of us born to my parents and raised out here on the Ferne Islands; and all are gone on, save Brooks and me, and this is how things will be. He to help Father, and by and by to be assistant lightkeeper, with a wage of his own; and I to help within. We will stay off; it is our fashion to call the mainland 'on' and the islands 'off'; we will stay off all our lives.

The morning before the melancholy shipwreck of the *Forfarshire*, Brooks would go into Sunderland. He had a barrel of herring to sell upon the quays, which he had taken with a babnet from the rocks we call Northern Hares. My mother had made a feather comforter too, to send to my married sister Betsy, on the main. So when William Swann, who is the boatman to the lighthouses – ours and the lighthouse on Inner Ferne – came out with a sack of dried peas and a letter from Thomasin, Brooks went away with him, promising to be home before nightfall. But as the wind got up in the day, and the sea took to jawing under a driving wind from northeasterly, it was plain he could not be back. He would be lodging with the Robson brothers, or with William Swann in Sunderland, and making the most of his chances in the beggar-maker's shop, with the money for his herrings in his pocket. We were not alarmed; though a tremendous blow was building up, we have sat through uncountable great storms, sitting by the fire, Father whittling or reading, and Mother and I knitting or spinning, and then two of us – never three, for at night someone must always be watching for a failure of the light – going to our curved bunks aloft in the blaring and wailing of the wind round the tower.

So there it was; with Brooks away, we made shift without him, and without him brought nine survivors to safety.

When Father came back from the wreck that second time, he sat a while drenched to the skin upon a barrel by the door, in a stun for weariness, and not ready to rouse himself and go aloft and fetch himself into dry clothes. Little time had passed since all were brought within; less than a half-hour certainly, when the sea began to beat up heavily against the door.

'Give me a hand once more, Tulloch,' said my father, 'and then you may rest your fill.' I could tell from the way he spoke that this man had Father's good opinion. They two got up, and struggled with the bar. We keep a baulk of oak as a bar, which drops into great iron brackets either side the door, and braces the door itself against the sea.

And no sooner was that done than there came a thunderous knocking *from outside*!

· 3 ·

I had not yet considered for a moment what might
be going forward on the mainland, though the Ferne
Islands lie full in view from the lookout at Balmboro'
Castle, and Mother had seen them send up the shipwreck flares. But later Thomasin told us how she
was woken from slumber at the first gleek of dawn
by the castle cannon firing. She jumped up, and
slipping on her mantle over her nightgown, looked
out through her casement window. The flag on the
castle was at half-mast, and there was a bustle begin-
ning of folk ganging down the street. The trees in
the grove between her cottage and the church were
thrashing about in the blast, and she shut up her
window quick enough. By the time she was dressed,
the word was running up and down between neighbours of a great ship wrecked on the Fernes, which
the castle watch had sighted, and thereupon roused
Mr Smeddle. Mr Smeddle is the only one of the
Crewe Trustees who lives at Balmboro', the others
all being at Durham or Newcastle, so it is he who
has all the managing of affairs; and he was said to be
gone at once to Sunderland on horseback to see to
the launching of the lifeboat.

Thomasin with some of the neighbours went

running up to the castle gate, from where there is a fine glower out seawards, and the Ferne Islands all lie in view.

'God preserve us!' she had said. 'That is terrible near to the Longstone; I fear me what my father and brother may design to do!'

And old Granny Cuthbertson, who was standing in the huddle of outlookers, all nearly blown off their feet, said, 'Divn't thee fret theesel, lass; thy brother is with my sons in Sunderland. Storm-stayed since yesternight. I seed him the'er mysel.'

Thomasin knew well that Father could do nothing by himself. She felt sorry for him, fretting at the spectre of wreck, and he helpless; but her fears for the safety of her family were quietened. She went home, and neatened her house, and mended her little fire, and took up her work, it being a gown for Mrs Smeddle, and sat by the window in clarty weather, and the light of morning darkening like dusk, and the rain coming on against the window-pane like a force in flood. And she was not fretting at all, she said, over us into danger, for she did not think any would be possible.

We heard later a great story from Brooks also, of what he had done that morning. He was full of the tale, and eager to spell it to us. He had been in Sunderland when Mr Smeddle came galloping up, somewhat out of breath from his ride, and began ordering good fellows around. All the able-bodied of the town, and all his boatmen bullies were out and about, for the high tide had washed right up to the row of cottages above the harbour, and floated off fish barrels from the little front crofts, and people were running about putting things in safety, and tying things down against what was to come on the next full tide, there being no sign of the wind letting up.

But news of a wreck upon the Fernes, and a splendid wreck too, soon took people's minds off fish barrels; a knot of folk gathered round Mr Smeddle, and the buzz was carried round by the scurrying small boys, bringing just about everyone out of their houses and to the quay.

There was a good deal of babblement and argufying, Brooks said. Mr Smeddle wanted a rescue tried, and, what was worse, he wanted the lifeboat launched for it. Now that lifeboat is a bone of contention between the gentry hereabouts, and the longshoremen. The lifeboat was built in London, and brought up here, given by the Duke of Northumberland, the great Duke at Alnwick. The Crewe Trustees at Balmboro' Castle look after it, just as they keep clothes and supplies for shipwrecked seamen, and fire guns, and post lookouts in storms. 'Into everything,' as Brooks says. William Robson is the lifeboat cox, and the fishermen can earn a shilling now and then taking the London boat out and practising with it. It's a little light bobbing thing. It hasn't the high, cutwater bows of a coble, and it hasn't the flat stern to smooth the rough water behind her, and it hasn't the great tiller, swimming deep below the stern; but it's supposed by the gentry to be better by far than just the cobles that northern folk pattern for themselves. Father says there was an 'inimmersible

boat' at Balmboro' when he was a youth; all
thwarted and lined with cork. That wore out shortly
with being launched and recovered on an open shore
– a beach knocks the bottom out of boats. And there
was a good lifeboat at Shields – called the *Original*,
was used for many years until it hit a rock some
eight years back and went to the bottom. Never lost
a man of its crews, all the years it was in service.
There's at least two dozen opinions over whether the
lifeboat at Sunderland is like the *Original*, or not so;
but there were only two opinions that morning about
whether the lifeboat could be got into the sea and
out to the Fernes or no; Mr Smeddle's, that it could,
and should, and everybody else's that it couldn't, and
would be overset at once in such a water.

Mr Smeddle was upset. 'Can nothing, nothing be
done?' he was crying.

'Such a Bob's-a-dying he set up as you never did
hear!' Brooks told us.

'Maybies there'll be help from the lighthouse?'
someone said. 'That's been known occasions before.'

'Darling can do nothing on his own,' said William
Swann. 'And Brooks is here.'

'Young Darling is here?' said Mr Smeddle.

'I couldn't get off last night,' said Brooks. He
thought Mr Smeddle was going to chide him for
being from home.

'Who is on the light?' said Mr Smeddle.

'Only my father, sir.'

'He is quite alone?'

'Except for the womenfolk. My mother and sister
are there.'

'The wreck seems to be on Harker Rock. What is that? Five or six cables from the lighthouse? It is not very far . . . could your father do anything?'

'The coble takes three good men in rough water, sir,' said Brooks. 'My father has no fool's head on his shoulders. He'll never stir.'

'So it is the opinion of you all that all are helpless, and no move can be made!' said Mr Smeddle. 'I cannot compel you. I suppose I may at least be thankful that what cannot be done for the sake of pity for our fellow men cannot be done for greed! I suppose there can be no looting in this weather!'

'Now don't take on, sir,' said Will Robson. 'We never said nothing could be done. We'll make an attempt – but in the soundest coble we can find; not in the lifeboat.'

'You'll risk your lives in a coble?' says Smeddle.

'Aw, let's be about it!' said Brooks, jumping into the coble at hand. There's six oars to a coble; he was followed fast by Thomas Cuthbertson, and William Swann, and three others. William Robson would be the tillerman, and he was held talking by Mr Smeddle.

'I just hope you know what you are doing!' said Mr Smeddle.

'We've got William Swann, the island boatman here, sir, and better yet, we've got a Darling too, that had the Fernes for calf-yard!' says Will Robson, and with that he gets to his tiller, and the boat pulls away.

They had five miles to row in direct line, right in the face of the storm. At the best of times it is a journey of a little more than an hour to make the distance into Sunderland; that morning they headed well north of north-easterly, to get into the lee of the Fernes as soon as they could. The waves were running towards them, and the wind tore at their backs, and struck into William Robson's face the whole way, and they were at their oars for near three hours before they reached the Harker Rock.

They were disappointed, of course, when they got there. The better part of the vessel was torn away and gone; the waves were breaking furiously over the remainder, and not a soul was found living in the melancholy scene. Only the bodies of children, and a poor clergyman, fretished to death with cold of the blast, were to welcome them. Those corpses they carried to a higher point, where Brooks reckoned they could not be washed off by the next tide; then they considered themselves.

They were in a tight corner. It had taken them much longer than they reckoned to reach Harker Rock; and it had been a brute of a row. For all their toughness and work-hardened bodies, they were tired. And by now the flood tide had come on, and was running hard against them. The wind had got up again, and the weather was furious. They did not at all like the look of the water; and as for rowing for maybe three hours, or perhaps four or five, against the tide, that would be chancy. That would be very hard, and they had spent the best of their strength already. It didn't take them long to think they would do better to get to the lighthouse instead. Even that was no easy matter. The tide was rising, and the shelter offered by the rocks was lessening minute by minute; the wind was howling and blaring through Crawford's Gut, and short though the distance was, the danger was enough to daunt them. And of course, Brooks told us bitterly, they were wet to the skin through their oilies, and bone-cold, and drawn by the hope of food and fire in our kitchen.

Even then it took them the better part of an hour to discover that they could not gain the shelter of the haven at Longstone; they simply had not strength enough to row themselves into the Sunderland Hole against the force of the storm. Now, Brooks said, they were very low in spirits. Each man knew well what peril they were in. For if they could not pull their boat into the Longstone haven, what likelihood was there of getting it back into harbour on the main? So with death staring at them they took a desperate chance; they rowed into the windward of the Longstone, and turned round to ride the waves towards the rocks; and a great breaker launched them over the rocks into a shallow on the ragged skerries where the Longstone Rocks run out beneath the sea at the southernmost end. The coble came down with great force, but she did not spring her boards. So they clambered out of her, and scarce able to stand in the teeth of the gale, they carried her over the rocks, with the sea clawing and frothering at their knees, and put her safely into the lee of a jutting rock at the Sunderland Hole. Then, staggering and buffeted and leaning against each other, their clothes being torn and whipping in the wind, they reached, as they thought, shelter; and finding the door barred, Brooks picked up a stone and hammered upon it, with all his remaining force.

· 4 ·

What terror the sound brought me, though of a moment's lasting!

For how could there be flesh and blood outside our wave-whelmed threshold, in the murderous thrashing of the sea? And if not flesh and blood, what spirit walked out there? When we were children we fancied the world of rock and water on which we lived to be full of ghostly things – drowned seamen, piteous and vengeful, that looked at us with seals' eyes from the heaving swell; or the wispy souls of monks and sinners drifting in the sea-fret, come seeking great Saint Cuthbert, and missing their way by a mile or so, and near a thousand years – for Cuthbert lives on the Inner Ferne, and every keeper of the light will confess to seeing him, when the storms are wild enough; T. Smith, who is the keeper there now, and our nearest neighbour, says he has seen the saint also on calm evenings, walking in a ragged robe at the water's edge of the little cove below the chapel ruin.

We took down the bar fast enough – Father and I and Mr Tulloch helping us. In my mind was a flurry of terrors and amazements; I suppose I did not really think of the ghosts of drowned men, though drowning was close to the grain of our thinking in that hour; but we would have said, I suppose, that we thought of the boats that might have been on the stern decks of the broken *Forfarshire*, and of the chance against chance that such a boat might have reached the Longstone Rocks ... Saint Cuthbert himself could not have astounded us more than Brooks did – Brooks and his bullies, drenched and wind-beaten, standing in the blast that the open door admitted.

It can but have been seconds, while time stood still, and we stared at each other. There was scarce room for them to step inside and let the door be closed; and when the door thudded to, and the uproar of wind entering abruptly ceased, they stood packed close, and dripping icy water on the flags of the floor, and I heard the clock ticking cumbrously while it dawned upon us that Father had been wrong; that the lifeboat *had* come out! And it dawned upon them that the strangers huddled to the warmth of the fire, all round the room, were those they had come to rescue.

Words stumbled at first.

'I swore you were alone; I swore you could do nothing ...' Brooks said to Father. 'How ... ?'

'Grace helped me,' Father said. 'I was dead sure the lifeboat could not get out ... how ... ?'

'Not the lifeboat! That pottle! But a coble. Has taken us since half of seven ...'

'Poor bodies!' my mother said. 'And how shall we do? With not a dry garment in the house, or a blanket to spare for you!'

My father had thrust his way to the little cupboard over the mantel, and fetched out the bottle of aqua vitae kept there for such throes as this. He unstoppered it, and held it out to William Robson. The bottle went from hand to hand. I think Father would not have let it pass from the lifeboat men to the shipwrecked, they being half warmed up, and all found in dry clothes, but he could not easily stop it, and it returned to him three-parts empty.

The liquor brought a flush back to frozen faces, and with it fired up bitter rage. William Robson – I shall ever remember it – leaned over the table towards Father, and brought his fist down crashing on the board, and cried out, 'You cormorant, Darling! You've filched every penny away from under our noses!'

And I swear with his words the first thought of the money at issue came to me; and brought a foreshadowing chill.

'You'll think better of that, man,' said Father calmly. 'What you have done in getting here, I judged impossible.'

'You judged it possible to get there first, you mean!' cried Robson. 'You greedy devil! Do you think we don't know what you get? Do you think we don't see what they send you – sacks of peas and sacks of flour, and salt and oil and rope and gear? Everything you need is found, and your wages over and above it! While we poor fellows labour for every ha'porth we eat, and must work for the least thing we need; and when here's a chance of a pawful of guineas between us – and dearly earned, and at our peril too – you sneak in there before us, and take all for yourself!'

Then William Swann spoke up. 'Your business is to keep the light, Darling; this was work of ours; and man's work, too – not fit for a girl. Shame on you, putting your daughter to it!'

Father said, very slowly and quietly, 'You are overweary, my bullies, and you speak in the heat of the moment. But, mind you, it is my roof you stand under, and I am the master here. You must bridle your tongues for as long as you shelter here. Do you mark me?'

'I'll see you in hell first!' cried William Robson. 'I'm not doffing my cap and come crawling to you! There's seven of us here and there's seven as good a man as you are, and will say what we please to say in all the world and any part o' Longstone! Bridle our tongues? Hold you the master while we shelter here?' He spat on the scrubbed board of the table. 'That's what we say to your shelter!'

And he struggled towards the door. We all were so crushed together in the space that he had to shoulder his way . . . he let the wind in again, howling; and brought a wail of dismay from our rescued visitors. Brooks looked about him distraught, and looked wildly at Father, and then he followed the boatmen out.

'What will they do?' said Mr Tulloch. 'Will they row to the mainland?'

'They'll drown if they try it,' said Father.

'Oh, Brooks . . .' said my mother in a fainting voice. 'Stop him, William!'

'I'll try to stop them if they go to the boat,' said Father, brushing the mist from the window, and looking out. 'But they will go to the barracks.'

'What are they?' asked Mr Tulloch.

'A rough shelter, thrown up for the masons when the lighthouse was being built,' Father told him.

'But the windows and doors are out, and the sea has taken off half the roof,' I said, grieving at the thought of it in the filth of the storm.

'Can this quarrel be mended?' asked Mr Tulloch.

'By and by it may be,' said Father. 'They are good brave fellows; I did not think they could do it.'

'What is this about money?' asked Mr Tulloch.

'You are worth a guinea a head,' Father told him. 'Being saved from a shipwreck.'

'It's more than we merit,' says Mr Tulloch. 'Who pays it?'

'The Crewe Trustees,' said Father.

'And who are they?' said Mr Tulloch.

I turned and stared at him. I was at the stove, stirring hasty pudding, for whatever the men might say to each other, warm food would be the difference between life and death in the barracks. Mother and I had silently set about making it. But I turned and stared with amazement that there could be someone from so far away that they did not know of the Crewe Trustees.

Father told him something about the great Lord Crewe, how he had died childless some hundred years since, and left his huge fortune in trust. How the Trustees prospered, running their vast estates, and how the money was spent on doing good, and looking after the people hereabouts. How the Trustees found jobs and schools and clothes for common folk, and, more to the point this moment, set up a multitude of measures against shipwreck — lookouts, and warning cannon, and rewards for attempts at rescue, and funds for the relief of those rescued, for new clothes for them, and money to see them home. I listened while Father talked, and Mr Tulloch in his turn told Father that in all England else there was no such thing; how the poor starved in the present hard times, and work was short, and bread dear, and the greater part of ordinary men could neither read nor write, for there was no teaching for them. I listened, but without stopping my tasks for a moment, so much was to do.

And what a pother we were in! Our discomfort was great, and we are little used to disorder within doors. Everything was wet. We strove mightily to dry clothes, but the dank of them having no way to go out, ran down the windows and lay in pools on the floors. We keep stock of clothing, and of bedding, but not by miles enough for such a throng of needy all at once. And even blankets were in shortage. The salt that came in on the garments of the poor drenched shipwrecked made everything tacky-damp, and our rooms stank like sea-wrack at low tide. The man called Donovan was so bruised about the legs and thighs that he could not move a muscle without pain, and could neither sit nor stand easily. He groaned a good deal. We did not yet know him for what he was, but took each and every one of our prizes as worthy our good opinion – they having all the great merit of their great misfortune.

Worse yet was the grief of Mrs Dawson. She was distracted; she wept and cried constantly for her bairns, poor lady, and tossed about in the narrow bed I had left for her. She could not help herself, but alas, she slept fitfully all day, and woke and wept at the descent of darkness, thinking herself still in the merciless blast of the storm – indeed the storm raged on, beating against the windows, and screaming round the tower, as though it were a wild creature howling after her. Who could blame her? Yet her grief and frenzy kept Mother and me from sleeping, for we had to put the three of us women all in one chamber, to leave room in the others for the men. In our life we do not sleep all night; someone must be in attendance every hour of darkness to mind the light, and we take shifts. But when we do sleep we sleep deeply, and from urgent need. Scant our sleep in those short hours when we are used to take it, and we are soon distraught, and hindered from our usual ways of working.

Then there was care for food. We keep stores; but to feed eighteen bodies, for none knew how long . . . There was bread flour, and dried peas, and oatmeal for porridge and hasty cakes; we had our home-cured salt-herring in a barrel, but while the storm blew we could not catch birds or fishes to help the pot, nor get to the Brownsman for rabbits or fresh greenstuff from the garden. The garden would be ruined, no doubt. We would have been well enough had we known we were besieged for three days; but it might have been three dozen for all that we knew; we doled out measured portions, and everyone was left with room for more.

But if we were in discomfort, think of those in the barracks, outside! We did think of them; as little by little we brought ourselves into some rough kind of comfort – warm at least, if not dry – they weighed each minute heavier upon our hearts. Father went out to them twice, hoping to talk them into coming in, but they would not heed him. Anger raged like the storm around them. Mr Tulloch went out to them later, trying what a stranger might do, and could do nothing. At five, when it must be that they would spend a night in the open unless they relented, my mother went out to them, with a pail of soup and hunks of hard bread, for which she got thank-you, but no change of answer as to taking shelter in the lighthouse. At last at dusk I went at Father's bidding, to bring them a tarpaulin and a bale of cord, that they might lash up some kind of shelter from the pelting rain.

They were all standing up against the wall, leaning together, for what warmth they had in their poor frozen bodies they were sharing. Brooks was tramping his feet, to keep the blood moving. Thomas Cuthbertson had no hat, and his face was tilted to the sky as he stood, eyes shut, head back, with the rain beating down his cheeks like tears, and his lips as blue as any corpse.

I grieved to see him so. And when I lay wakeful and tired out upon the floor that night, it was Thomas I fretted over, to be truthful, as much as

Brooks. Cuthbertsons are nothing to me; but young Thomas once handed me ashore from William Swann's boat, when I went to bide a week with Thomasin. As he gave me his hand to help me up the ladder from the boat he said to me softly, 'Lass, thou's mayed to my fancy . . .' I made no answer, only to glim at him a moment. But this I remembered, and this made me pity him, now.

Mine is the watch at first light. From the lantern floor at dawn I saw them moving from the barracks, struggling out against the wind, putting the coble into the heaving water in Sunderland Hole, and rowing away, Brooks with them. They were quick about it. By the time I had roused Father, which I did by going to his side and shaking him by the shoulder, for calling to him would have woken all our sleepers, they were launched, and beyond call. They went on the ebbing tide, which would draw them away from the islands.

'Can this be wise?' I asked Father.

'It's reckless, rather,' he said. 'I would have thought Swann at least more careful.'

'Brooks knows better,' I said. 'What is Brooks thinking of?'

'He is thinking of helping his mates get out of what scrape he helped them into,' said Father sharply. 'That's plain, girl.'

So I knew from his tone with me that he was worried for Brooks. And indeed, this time we were right to think their attempt impossible; they were driven back, coming in again two hours later, and finding it as hard as ever to get their coble into safety.

We took food to them at midday, and again at five, when we were making a meal for the strangers. Brooks took dried driftwood from the store, and made them a fire in an old bucket, and they stood round it in a corner of the masonry where the walls were highest. We did not bar the door, nor cease to fret over them.

And later Brooks told me how, in the night – it was during Father's watch, for I was fast asleep – the tide with the wind behind it washed into the barracks, and put out the fire. They were standing in the sea to their knees, and the slap and knock of the waters threatening to drag them over. Above their heads the sweep of the light showed them as it passed, though dimly through the beating rain, the plight of the others. The young men were faring worse; the older more inured to hardship; but by then, Brooks said, they were all in a pretty bad way. Brooks was leaning face to the wall, against a glassless window, through which the wind blew in at him, but the sill gave a purchase for his elbows to lean upon, and ease his weary legs, and his feet numbed in his seaboots, which had filled with water. He thought he was seeing things, for a will-o'-the-wisp came glimmering to and fro across the rocks. He rubbed the rain out of his eyes with his hands, and looked again, and he seemed to see a jack o' lantern carried towards him, and floating above it a ghost of his father's face. 'I thought I was gone over,' he told me, 'and that death had come to fetch me.' Then the light and the vision disappeared both at once, and while he stood mazed and wondering, suddenly he heard Father's voice behind him.

Father was standing beside the sodden ashes of the fire-pail. He had taken his place beside William Robson. He had put down his lantern, propped himself against the wall, turned up his collar, and pulled his storm bonnet down, as though he had settled there.

'This is a bad business, William,' he said.

Robson made him no answer. 'They tell me they had no warning in the steerage, nor any chance to take to the boats, but the first they knew of danger was the breaking open of their cabins to the sea. They tell me she was not fit to sail, and her boilers were already giving trouble before she left Hull. That and a lot beside. If they are right, what they say, then there is little hope for the passengers in the stern. Most likely they never got into boats, and if they did, I don't reckon their chances were high of making landfall.'

Robson still said nothing. Father went on, Brooks said, speaking in a level tone, as though to himself, though he had need to raise his voice against the gale. 'Only nine living from not less than sixty souls, I think. Tulloch is a good man; he got twelve from the wreck on to the rocks, but the bairns and the clergyman died of the cold before morning. One would expect it; the gentry have no strength in hardship, and the bit bairns were thin and peaky. A working man has more marrow in him. A working man can last longer. Not for ever though.'

There was a long silence then, in which Brooks and the others all looked at Robson.

Robson said, 'Get yow in, Darling. There's no call for you to be here.'

Father said, 'I'll stand out while you stand out, I think.'

'Please yourself,' said Robson.

They stood silent long enough for Father to be drouked to the skin like the rest. Father never caught Brooks's eye. Brooks said he was in mortal fear that Father would order him within, and make a breach between him and his bullies that would last a lifetime. But Father did no such thing. In a while he said, 'This is a wanchancy thing altogether, Robson. A bad business. And we look set to make it worse. Let us cry barley-bay, and you come in.'

'I'm no coming bin a house where I canna speak my mind,' said Robson.

'Say what you will,' said Father, 'but say it soft, and dinna let's have the strangers stirring. We've enough to do looking to them all the day long.' Still he had no answer. 'Is it the thought of the premiums channering at yow? Yous'll have your due, man, you and all these, if I have any doing with it,' said Father.

'Barley, then,' said Robson.

So when Father roused me, on his way to his bunk, and when I had got off the shakey-down on the floor where I was sleeping fitfully, and gone up to quench the light, I descended to the kitchen and found it packed like a herring barrel, with my brother and his bullies taking turns to press up close to the fire. I made up hasty cakes for breakfast, saying nothing about the meagre quantity of meal remaining in the sack. I could barely move about my task, till three of the men removed themselves to squat upon the barrels in the oil-store. And if I was weeping as I worked it was from pure relief.

That was a bad morning. It was all we could do to keep from snapping at each other as we tripped over feet, and shouldered each other trying to move by to get a thing done. There were bodies and bundles everywhere, everyone cramped and desperate, and the air dank and stale. Mr Donovan howled and swore when someone jostled his hurt legs, but it was a mishap, while a body stepped aside to let Mother pass to the foot of the stair with a pannikin of hot water to take up to Mrs Dawson.

'Shut thy mouth, Donovan!' the man cried. 'I'm sick to my stomach listening to yow!' We thought that he meant he had enough of such swearing noise-making; later I knew better. But howbeit, Mr Tulloch soothed them down, and said to Father, 'We have all got cabin-fever, Darling, shut up here as in a ship with no decks.'

'It can happen we are closed in for a month together,' Father said. 'But it takes some getting used to, we know.'

'Ah, how do you bear it?' another man said. 'It was thronged enough while these latest were outside . . .'

'Time to dance,' said Father, taking his fiddle case off its hook beside the mantel.

'You're mad, Keeper,' someone said. 'Dance, when we have no room to breathe?'

'On your feet,' said Father, looking up from tuning his strings. 'And up the stairs. Up the stairs, round the rooms, and up the stairs again, and round the light, and down again. And all in step, and all in time. Gracie leads off; Gracie cow-leading; Gracie will show you! And *one*, and *two*, and . . . !' And Father struck up 'Smash the Windows' with gusto. We had to chivvy them at first. They were so stiff they could scarce dance a step.

'Will you make fools of us?' said one of the life-boat bullies.

'Never, friend,' Father said, not breaking off the ditty. 'This is in earnest. *For your life* – dance, will you!' And soon we were skipping in a long line up the stairs, and 'Smash the Windows' was sounding cheerfully from top to bottom of the light, as Father brought up the end of the line. Next he played 'New Gravel Lane', and 'Devil among the Tailors' and 'Push about the Jorum', and kept us moving, moving. When someone cried enough, and called their weariness he scolded them on, saying who stopped first had least dinner to expect. And when at last the fiddle fell silent, and the dance was halted, it was as we had often found it, from our childhood, when Father danced us on clarty days – everyone found their limbs warmed and their minds more cheerful. And as all returned to their barrel, or stool, or scrap of standing room, suddenly the sun came clear, and shone in through the dirty windows, and then men began to rub the glass and blink out, and talk of a chance of going.

· 5 ·

It was about noon when the wind eased off some-what. It had ripped every cloud out of the heavens, and the sea was heaving mightily under a thin blue sky. William Robson reckoned he might get back, not without an effort, he knew, but at least his men were warm and dry, and we none of us thought the easing of the wind could be relied upon to last. We would all be hungry by tomorrow unless they could get away, for all our stores were at bottom now. The men conferred together, needs must all in on the talk, for we had standing-room only in the kit-chen. The lifeboat bullies made up their minds to try it for a mile, and turn back if they were forced to it. Father needed to go with them, to reach Balm-boro' with news, and arrange relief for our guests. But with Father going, Brooks had need to stay, for someone must be answerable for the light. For the work of it, I could have done it, but the rules are strict about keeping shifts, and forbid one person from taking two shifts one after other.

'As for sparing Brooks, and having you take his oar, Darling,' said Robson, 'are you as strong as he?'

'It's young Cuthbertson who's in the poorest way,' said William Swann. 'He hurt his ankle and skinned his shins when we were putting the boat over the rocks. Take Brooks and Darling both, and leave Cuthbertson.'

'He has no knowledge of the light,' said Father.

'He can see if it is working or not,' said Robson. 'And wake Grace to see to it if owt's amiss.'

My father looked across to me, and I nodded to him. 'Let's be going then,' Father said.

When they were gone, Thomas Cuthbertson and I climbed to the lantern to watch the attempt, and soon we saw the coble going bravely away from us, bucking over the waves' backs, and already pulled well off the rocky edges of the islands, though making in the lee of the stacks.

'That's a dandy, then,' he said, 'if the surf is slacking.'

'That we cannot see from here,' I told him. A soft surf and a violent one make both alike the faintest line of white from where we stand. 'Now, what is this about a hurt to your leg?'

'Nothing to fret about with so much amiss,' he said.

'Let me see.'

He showed me a gruesome wound running the length of his shin, and swollen all about the knee. I took him to my room, paying no heed to intruding upon Mrs Dawson, and brought the medicine-box there, and cleaned and salved the wound, at which he flinched a little. 'You should not have been standing on this,' I told him. 'It is all soft and sodden with being wet so long, and may not knit again. No wonder they would leave you.'

'Give over, Gracie,' he said. 'I'm not the first in need round here.' And he looked at me slyly to see if I would bridle at being called Gracie, which I scorned to do.

As to injuries of the spirit, Mrs Dawson was truly the first in need. She could not yet pay any mind to any other soul, or any happening around her. As to injuries of body, truth was Mr Donovan was the worst hurt by far. It was Mr Donovan also who had most to tell. He was the one who told us the terrible story of the disaster, and of the wickedness of the Captain. For it seemed that the *Forfarshire* had left the Humber in an unfit state, and all should have known better than to take her to sea in such a way, so that the loss of lives aboard her amounted to little less than murder. So Mr Donovan held. Mr Donovan's legs were bruised and torn as he struggled in the twisted wreckage to get himself free and down upon the rock; he was bad enough hurt to have unquestioned claim on the best place we could give him, and since he could not go upon his feet, and it is not easy to carry a man up a narrow spiral stair wide enough for only single file, we had given him the settle in the kitchen for a bed, making it up with blankets, and a pillow, so that he was warm and close to the fire, and seeing and hearing all that went on around him. There he chipped in to every conversation, and his story was woven into everyone's view of the calamity.

Mr Donovan told us that before ever the *Forfarshire* left the Humber – before ever she reached the open sea – he would have given everything he possessed to be off her, to be back in port and in safety. He said that her boilers were not in fit condition, and that the Captain knew it. He talked at great length of the luxury of the passenger cabins and staterooms on the *Forfarshire*; of her services of fine plates and silver for the dining-room; of the mahogany and brass and crystal chandeliers in her saloons. 'No money spared, friends,' he told us, 'on anything that showed – but you should have seen the chaos below decks! The accommodations in the steerage were a scandal! The engines and boilers were neglected and the engineer grudged even an oil-can to keep things greased! Yet anyone could guess how a paddle steamer would fare without power! The company are guilty of murder, of murder no less!'

'Her boilers were fixed before we left Hull, Donovan,' said one of the seamen. 'A number of rivets was refastened, and we got up steam and found the boilers sound before she slipped hawsers and set sail.'

'Botched! Scrimped and botched!' said Mr Donovan.

'Why do you say so?' asked the seaman. 'You wasn't there yet; you hadn't come aboard yet, and you wouldn't have come at all if it had been up to me!'

'Had you kept me off her I would have owed you a heavy debt,' said Mr Donovan. 'And I say the repairs were botched because all was wrong again within hours, that's why. Of course it was botched.'

'Engineer was satisfied. I heard him say so,' muttered the seaman.

'The engineer?' said Mr Donovan scornfully. 'In

51

league with the Captain, sir. I have not a doubt of it.'

'Remember, Donovan, the Captain had his wife with him,' Mr Tulloch struck in.

'I don't forget it!' Mr Donovan said. 'He was grudging to pay her coach fare to Dundee, no doubt, if he had to postpone sailing. Sparing his private pocket at risk of all our lives!'

At that another man of the crew spoke up – it was almost the first thing I had heard him say – he said, 'I saw the Captain go – I saw him taken from the deck by a great wave –' He paused, seeming overcome.

'What difference does it make if you saw him or no?' said Mr Donovan. 'He had lost his ship by his folly, before that.'

'He and she was gone together. He had his arms round his wife . . .'

One of the passengers, a weaver from Dundee, said then, 'We should not speak ill of the dead, Mr Donovan.'

'Should we not?' cried Mr Donovan, now very wrought up. 'Do you think it is down to us to say who is at fault in this calamity? The powers of the land will want to dispose of this! There'll be inquests to be held and inquiries, perhaps, and I'll speak up fearlessly and tell the truth from end to end of England, so I will, and never let fear of speaking ill of the dead constrain me! And I'll call you all to witness what I say!'

'So be it, if it be the truth you speak,' said Mr Tulloch. 'But the most of us here work for the company, and will be paid and employed again by them. There will be no call for us to say that the company let the *Forfarshire* go out without her boilers being seen to, when we all know it was done.'

'Ah, there's the worm in the biscuit, though – I see it now!' said Donovan. 'You all work for the company, and will be muzzled like dogs. But I don't; not any more. I'm a free man, and they cannot silence me. They'll live to regret dismissing me!'

'It was the purser's fault you were allowed to work for a free passage back to Dundee – and he hasn't lived to regret it, God rest his soul,' said Mr Tulloch. 'I'd have left you rotting in Hull; you're a trouble-maker. Always were.'

'Well, you've an axe of one kind to grind, and I've an axe of another. What do passengers think – what do you think, James Kelly?'

'I know nothing of seafaring. I have been through hell,' said Mr Kelly quietly, 'and I have no opinion about it. Except perhaps that it is poor thanks to the young woman who rescued us, and her family, to disturb her quiet with quarrelling.'

'What do you think?' Mr Donovan asked, turning next to the oldest of those we had rescued. 'You've been longer than any of us at sea.'

'I think that old sail was safer than this new steam,' said this man. 'Nothing ever befell me in a clipper as bad as struggling below deck with a bilge full of scalding hot water slapping around.'

'But do you think it was the company's fault?' said Mr Donovan.

'I don't know, friend,' was the answer he got, 'and neither, I think, do you.'

You may imagine with what attention my mother and I listened to these exchanges. If any had indeed been at fault, we too had been put at risk thereby, and all the stout fellows from the Sunderland lifeboat crew. But I could not make it out. Mr Donovan spoke with an Irish lilt, and most gentlemanly and fluently in his manner of speech, though he was but a common man in manners and in dress; the others were all plain working men, the seamen in lowly trades, Tulloch, a carpenter, being the best of them for rank, the three trimmers being only seaborne labourers. These others spoke as plainly as they looked; they would have made no match for Mr Donovan in any war of words, and I inclined towards their way of thinking. But I was not used to prating. I could not believe Mr Donovan was not telling truth, and if he was he was surely very right in his great anger at the company.

Even with Father gone, and the lifeboat bullies also, there were twelve of us still on the Longstone to be fed, from the very little food left. Upon Mother and I wondering what might remain in our garden on the Brownsman, Thomas Cuthbertson and Mr Tulloch offered to row me over in the coble to recover what we could. Much would be ruined by blown salt, and the wind would have stolen away soil so laboriously built up there by our unremitting toil over the years. We carry seaweed from the shores to rot upon the ground within the circle of the garden walls; the sea takes back a deal of what it gives us, every year. But there might be cabbages and leeks and some potatoes recoverable. The storm would have uprooted them and laid them down upon the ground, but they can be gathered and washed before they rot.

We left Mr Tulloch upon Big Harker as we went, he wishing to inspect the wreck closely; and Thomas Cuthbertson and I went on to the Brownsman together. There I winced to see what a waste our ground was in. Thomas tried to shoot a few rabbits with Father's gun, while I filled a sack with taties and cabbage and leeks. I sang as I worked, the open air and the bright weather lifting my spirits high. When we were done all we could we ran right round the garden to stretch our legs and fill our lungs with air, and we were blithe enough as we rowed back.

'Yow wasna' scarit, Gracie, rowing by here in sic' a blow?' Thomas asked me.

'I was scarit,' I answered him, mimicking his voice. 'Do you think I'm daft?'

He laughed. 'Yow row like a bully, and sing like a linnet, Gracie,' he said. 'But your father kens well Harker is Sunderland territory.'

I did not attend to his meaning, for a big wave rolled out of nowhere and struck the coble, so then we saved our breath, for the wind was boisterous still, and the thwacking water fought our oars all the way home. Our laughing mood did not stay with us long; when we took up Mr Tulloch from Big Harker he was long-faced and queasy-looking. He had found a body in the wreck. I have seen a three-day drowned man once myself, and I could not blame him.

· 6 ·

Thomasin told me how while we were pent up in the lighthouse, a mighty uproar swept over those on the main. From daybreak on Friday the masts and forepart of the *Forfarshire* had been visible from Balmboro', and even from Sunderland; the towns were thronged with folk from far and near, sea-gazing. There was no news; and the whole of Sunderland was wringing hands over the lifeboat crew, who had gone out and not come back again. Bad though these poor men had fared for cold and hunger in the time, their kindred feared far worse; their mothers and sisters were weeping silently behind closed doors. About three in the afternoon on Saturday a copy of the *Gateshead Observer* was brought into Balmboro' from a traveller on the Great North Road, which passes some five miles inland from the town; it was a special edition of the paper, printed to carry news of the disaster. And what news it had was of the *Forfarshire*'s quarter-boat, which had been lowered, and taken on nine men, and then by some miracle had been swept away through the rocks to the open sea, where it had been sighted and picked up by a Montrose sloop, which had brought the men in it into Shields, and landed them safely. They could say nothing of the fate of any passengers other than a Mr Ritchie, and could confirm but few names of those whom they had seen board the ship. The relatives of anyone who was journeying in the north, and who might possibly have boarded the *Forfarshire* in Hull, were frantic for any news, good or ill. The paper printed a rumour that the ship was grounded on the Fernes, and a number of passengers were safe – though everyone in Balmboro' knew the thing was not, could not be, known.

Thomasin walks out every day, to fill her lungs with clean air, and rest her eyes a little from the close work of her sewing. Father most strictly ad-monished her to do so, for we know too many dressmakers near blind in their old age. But for those three days she was breaking off at the end of near every seam, and running down the street to the castle, and up on to the green before the gatehouse, from which a wide sweep of sea is in prospect, and the Ferne Islands can be seen, and where an agitated crowd was watching and using spy-glasses every hour of every day. Mr Smeddle's servants were riding the three miles to Sunderland, to and fro, and five miles to the Great North Road, where six coaches a day go past, bringing news, or rather not bringing any, for none was to be had.

None that is, until a castle-groom rode in with a young man riding pillion behind him, who no sooner dismounted than he began talking. Mr Smed-dle came out to him, and everyone crowded round eagerly, and Thomasin, who had just come up for the third time that day, was among the throng. The newcomer was Mr Ritchie, and he had come, he said, to discover what had become of his uncle and aunt. There was some confusion before he made himself plain, but soon it was understood that he had been a passenger on the *Forfarshire*, and the only one who had been in the quarter-boat; the other eight had all been of the crew.

Mr Smeddle, Thomasin said, had been trying to usher Mr Ritchie within the castle, to make a full report of himself in private; but when it became clear from his words – he was very excited, and pouring out his heart to the bystanders – that he alone from among the passengers had contrived to get into the boat, Mr Smeddle put on a very grave and serious face, and ceasing to try to draw him away from the crowd, began instead to invite him to tell his story to 'all these witnesses, my good neighbours'.

Thomasin noticed particularly, she told me, with that funny wry face she pulls, for though she had for long been a neighbour of the castle, this was the first time she had been advanced to a good neighbour, and certainly the first time she had been a witness to any matter of moment.

Mr Ritchie then took breath, and told his story. He had been below deck, as had all the cabin passengers, for the storm was fearful, and everyone was frightened and sick. Mr Ritchie's cabin was just at the foot of the companion-way, and at some distance from the cabin shared by his uncle and aunt. Sometime during the hours of darkness he heard suddenly the Captain's voice crying down the stairwell, 'On deck! Abandon ship!' Hearing this, he had leapt from his bunk in his underwear, and began to scramble up the steps; then, he said, he had remembered his trousers, and gone back for them. He raced back, and seized his trousers, and then, not stopping to put them on, he had struggled to the deck – the water was washing over the vessel and coming down the companion-way in torrents – and he had then struggled around on the deck, which was sloping terrifyingly, until he had seen on the forequarter the boat being lowered, and clutching his trousers tightly to his chest he had jumped into it.

'He said,' Thomasin reported, smiling in spite of herself, ' "Oh sirs! Had I stopped to put on my trousers, I shudder to think what would have become of me!" '

'It's certainly very strange,' I offered, 'that a man who thinks highly enough of his trousers to go back for them at risk of his life, should have thought not highly enough of them to put them on!'

'Why, but all his money was in the pockets!' Thomasin said. 'Didn't I mention that? It was only because of those trousers he was able to appear before us decently clad in a new suit of clothes.'

Mr Ritchie's trousers may have given us a smile, but the rest of his story was clearly no laughing matter. He was frantic with anxiety about his uncle and aunt, what had become of them, and at first had difficulty in understanding that the people pressing around him had no news to give.

He was led, Thomasin told me, to the brink of the precipice on which the castle stands, and a dozen hands pointed him in the direction to look out, and see the Fernes in their fairest aspect on a fine bright day, with the white horses galloping all over the sea, and the wreck clearly visible – and seeing it he was greatly dismayed, and was comforted, with some difficulty, by a swig of rum from Mr Smeddle's hip-flask.

At last he stopped saying, 'Oh, my poor uncle! Oh, my poor, poor aunt!', and paid some mind to Mr Smeddle.

'Are we to understand you, sir, that the crew of the doomed vessel made no attempt to save any of the passengers, but heartlessly made off in the boat themselves?' Mr Smeddle asked him.

'There was so little time . . .' Mr Ritchie said. 'The Captain called out . . . I think I was the only one who heard him.'

'But howsoever, the fact is that you were the only passenger to be taken into the boat, and your presence in that boat was due to your own efforts entirely.'

'Certainly,' said Mr Ritchie.

'Nobody, to your certain knowledge, made any attempt to rescue you, or anybody else. Nobody directed you to the boat, and invited you to get into it.'

'No, indeed,' Mr Ritchie said. 'I saw the boat being lowered, and I jumped in.'

'That is all I require to know of you, sir,' said Mr Smeddle. And to the crowd he said, 'Shocking! Horrid and shocking! Those wretches deserted their duty and left all but this poor gentleman to drown!

And now they are gone back to the company, we understand, all ready to fudge up some story or other to account for it all, before even the truth of the disaster can be known to any of us!'

'Well, they work for the company, sir; 'tis to be expected they will look to their employer's interest,' said the castle-groom.

He got a murmur of agreement from the crowd. 'He was as good as saying,' Thomasin opined, 'that none of us would dare do other than what we supposed the Crewe Trustees would wish for. Had Mr Smeddle been caught out in some dreadful deed . . .' – here she paused, being overcome with laughter at the thought – 'everyone in Balmboro' would run about standing by him, whatever their secret thoughts on the matter might be.'

Mr Smeddle, however, had not seemed to understand that his audience, who all owed their security and the bread in their children's mouths to the good opinion of a great man – or a great committee, rather – would sympathize with others who, owing their jobs and prospects to a shipping company, might consider what they said about the shipwreck of a company vessel. The Crewe Trustees are father and mother to the people of Balmboro': they give them work and schooling, and help their sons into useful lives and their daughters into respectable marriages, and see to the poor and the sick, and the shipwrecked. They are father and mother to the people, and the people are therefore their children.

Mr Smeddle though, seemed not to realize that the groom had reminded everyone what freedom of

61

thought a working man might have before the gentry; 'Interests of the company!' he shouted. 'We'll give them interests of the company! The truth is what we'll have, my friends! They'll not find it so easy to bamboozle Balmboro'!'

'If Uncle and Aunt are drowned indeed, they'll have me to reckon with,' added Mr Ritchie, still tremulous.

'The poor gentleman is in need of some care, sir,' said a woman in the crowd, and Mr Smeddle recollected himself, and took Mr Ritchie within.

Thomasin went home to her sewing, to take her mind off her fears for Brooks; but the crowd still lingered, hungrily scanning the windlashed shore and seascape, and the distant view of the Fernes, as though the view itself might at any moment give news of poor Uncle and Aunt, and so many others astray.

I had to admit to Thomasin that what with all the to-do on the Longstone, and so many to feed and care for, and so little elbow room, I had never given a moment's thought to the distress on the main where folk had less news than we had; and precious little thought had I given to the fate of the others on the vessel, and what numbers of them there had been.

Balmboro' Church was packed to the doors on Sunday. Praying had never been so popular, Thomasin said. From the church, folk flocked to the shore again to keep up their watch, and the sea being somewhat calmer, and the air clear, they were rewarded at last by those who had use of a spy-glass crying that they could see a boat making away from the outer islands. The neighbours all knew that no boat could land on the roaring beach at Balmboro', and being full of hope against hope that the boat might be the lifeboat crew's coble from Sunderland, not lost after all, the crowd thronged eagerly along the road to Sunderland, running and babbling, and arrived there the three-mile distance at about the same time that the boat drew in sight of Sunderland and a like excitement broke out there. Mr Smeddle and Mr Ritchie, astride a castle horse, went galloping past the crowds as they thronged past St Aidan's Dunes, and were on the Sunderland dock before them.

The whole town came out for their bully boatmen, and lined every yard of quayside, every inch of vantage point, and stood silent as death as they saw what trouble the boat was in. As the boat drew close inshore, all could see how the huge surf tossed and worried it. Over and over again a great wave swept it from sight, and thrust it up in view again, to a sighing from the crowd like the inland wind in the treetops.

For nearly an hour the people watched the boat in peril. The swell was heaving and crashing in the little harbour, and great waves were engulfing the break-water at every seventh throw. And all the while a retired sea captain, who drank in the Ship, and knew every soul in Sunderland, bent his powerful spy-glass on the boat, catching and losing it constantly in the bucking waters, but straining hard to see if he could, who was in it.

Only when the bullies gave up trying to get in at Sunderland, and turned the boat's head out to sea again, could the captain see the faces of the draggled men at the oars. He called out the names in his great storm-roaring voice, bringing joy and fear at once to the bystanders. He had seen James and Michael Robson, and William Swann, and William Robson – he could not tell who was at the helm.

'Oh, but just think, Gracie, think, Mother,' Thomasin told us, 'with what terror I heard him call out that there were Darlings in the boat – "The boy and his father," as he said.'

Meanwhile the boat struggled on, drawing out of range of the captain's glass, strong though it was, and was rowing southwards, towards Beadnell, where a jut of the coast might give shelter enough to come in. The crowd went streaming away on the Beadnell road, all ganging southwards, full of fear where the dunes broke their view of the sea, though Mr Smeddle as he passed could tell them, from his saddle, that he still had it clear in view, and it was still afloat.

So at last the boatmen came home, beached in Beadnell harbour, and the folk of three towns stood packed like barrelled herrings to greet them. Their path was barred by the crowd, and Mr Smeddle, standing foursquare, demanding news.

'There are nine saved,' said William Robson.'And three found dead – a grown man and two bairns.'

'Only nine!' cried Mr Smeddle. 'Out of so many!'

'Nine better then none, sir,' William Robson said. 'Darling is come to make report of them.'

'I want the fullest possible report from every one of you . . .' Mr Smeddle said.

'We have been without shelter the better part of three days and nights,' Robson said. 'We are bone-frozen, and famished, and dog-weary. For God's mercy, sir, bring us indoors, and to fires and food and dry clothing, and leave reporting till later!'

At that, of course, each man's family rushed forwards, each man's arms were drawn across his brothers' or his cousins' or his neighbours' shoulders, Beadnell people were throwing open their doors, offering their suppers and their beds, and their best Sunday clothing . . .

Above the hubbub of voices Mr Smeddle called out to William Robson, '*Why* were you without shelter, and hungry, Robson?'

He made a hush, Thomasin said – she had just thrust her way through to Brooks's side when he spoke – as everyone lingered a moment to hear the answer.

'The rescued were there before us, and the light-house thronged,' Robson said. 'The Darlings did all they could, and we managed with what there was, and we have no complaint.'

Mr Smeddle might have asked further, Thomasin said, had poor Mary Cuthbertson not made a diversion, by shrieking at William Robson to know what had become of Thomas, and falling in a faint on being told he was safe at the lighthouse. Then several Cuthbertson cousins at Beadnell sought to have Father and Brooks come in to their fireside for comfort, and Mr Smeddle said it would be as well, and

65

he would ride back to the castle, and send a coach to bring Father and Brooks, and Thomasin alongside them, to the castle, where they could be comfortably lodged, and tell him all they had to tell.

'He is kind enough when you nudge him to it,' Thomasin says.

In all this everyone had forgotten about Mr Ritchie. He followed Father within the little house, and pulling gently at his sleeve to have his attention he named his uncle and aunt, and asked if they were among the nine rescued.

'I am afraid not,' Father said. 'I much regret it . . .'

Mr Ritchie went out into the little garth behind the house, and sat down on an upturned barrow, and put his head in his hands, and wept bitterly for as long as it took the coach to come from Balmboro'.

· 7 ·

On Monday the dawn came bright and quiet. The
wind had dropped, so that as I quenched the lamps
and scanned the points of the compass for shipping
to enter in the keeper's log, the only sound I heard
was Mrs Dawson weeping in my room below. And
the swell was subsiding at last, so that I thought
with much relief that Father and Brooks would get
back to us, and the strangers might be taken onshore,
and we have some provisions made good.

And my hopes were met; before eight in the
morning a boat came out to us, bringing supplies
from the agent in Sunderland of flour, oatmeal, dried
peas, sugar, tea and coffee, and gifts from various
friends also – a chicken and some hens' eggs from
Mary Cuthbertson, and a basket of apples from the
castle gardeners, and a pottle of blackberries picked
by Sunderland children – all fresh, tempting things,
from which Mother and I prepared a great late breakfast, to fortify our hungry guests against passage in
the open boats.

An hour later the customs officer at Balmboro'
came out in a fishing-smack to visit the wreck, and
then came on to us, and ate heartily of the mountain
of hasty cakes we had been making; and he had

hardly finished his coffee, what with lingering to hear what the rescued had to tell him, than a Mr Sinclair arrived, coming direct from Berwick in a fast launch, likewise wishing to inspect the wreck, being the Lloyd's agent.

With gentlemen such as these to deal with, we heartily wished for Father to return to us, but though it could not be long, he was not with us yet. Mr Sinclair wished to know at what time the wreck was first sighted, and in what condition it then was, and learning that I had first seen it he made that an excuse to lead me up to the lantern floor, and show him exactly how I had come to see it.

It was only an excuse; he wished to speak to me out of earshot of the crowd of folk below. 'You seem a sensible enough young person, Miss Darling,' he said to me. I dropped him the ghost of a curtsy. 'You have been closely confined with these people for the space of three days.' I nodded. 'No doubt you have formed an opinion as to which of them is a reliable and steady sort of man?'

'I must admit I had not considered it,' I told him. 'They are all alike distressed and in need.'

'Of course, of course they are. Sentiments do you credit. But I am responsible to the insurers of the ship, who will be liable for very large sums of money, Miss Darling; more money than you can dream of . . .'

'I understand that, sir. I do not dream of money.'

He smiled. 'I am sorry, Miss Darling. I do not mean to impugn your character. The fact is that I must appoint one of the men below to the office of agent for the owners, to keep an eye on the wreck. Mr Donovan thrusts himself on my attention the most prominently; he has a lot to say, and seems a confident sort of man.'

'Sir, I think you should know that Mr Donovan had been dismissed by the company. We understand he was on board by the charity of his former ship-mates, and no longer as an employee.'

'Indeed?'

'I do not know if he was justly dismissed, or for what offence. It is not my business to wonder. But I do not think he is a friend of the owners.'

'Thank you for telling me this. Is there someone more suitable, to your mind?'

'I feel that I cannot say. It is a short and slight acquaintance we have with any of them, in circumstances of great trial. But if Father were here, I think he would recommend Mr Tulloch to your notice.'

'Which is he?'

'He is the ship's carpenter. I believe he has worked for the company for some time.'

'Thank you very much, Miss Darling. You have been of the greatest possible assistance to me.' Saying this he looked at me, I thought, unnecessarily sharply, and continued, 'If only my own daughters . . . your hermit's life out here must have been bracing to your sense . . .'

Later I told Father about this conversation. 'You did very well, Gracie,' he told me. 'Mr Donovan lodged with us indefinitely would have tried our patience sorely!'

'But Father . . .'

'Nay Gracie, I mean it. You said just the right thing.'

'I am glad of it. But what meant he, do you think, about his daughters?'

'Why Gracie, surely we haven't kept you so far cut off from common life that you haven't heard of silly young women with their heads full of hat-feathers?' he said, laughing.

But as I said to Thomasin when we talked it over – sooner or later we two talk over everything that befalls either one of us – I have heard mocking talk about women, true enough. But the women I know are a practical, sensible sort for the most part; it's the young men's heads that I know that fill up with moonshine as quickly as a leaking coble with water.

Father and Brooks came at around midday. They came in the castle boat, bringing Mr Smeddle himself, and a throng of reporters from the *Berwick Advertiser*, and other papers. There was great confusion, everyone talking at once, and trying to put their stories forward for the attention of the newcomers. Mother and I were busied to put food and drink from our shrinking new supplies before any guest or visitor – we would think shame to do otherwise – and Father was busy with recovering the bodies from Big Harker, and stowing them well out of sight before the shipwrecked, and Mrs Dawson in particular, were invited to board the boat to go into Sunderland. Mother said, 'Leave the bodies be, and see to the living,' but Father said Mr Smeddle was most eager to have the bodies landed, to have an inquest as soon as possible. 'Yes indeed –

before the codding and blame-shifting begins!' said Mr Smeddle, overhearing us.

The reporters were busily writing down everything Mr Donovan said about the state of the boilers. And then they began to ask who had been taken off the rock by the Sunderland boat.

'The lifeboat?' cried Mr Donovan. 'We saw neither hair nor hide of *them* till the danger was over!'

'It was the Darlings brought us to safety,' Mr Tulloch said.

'Picture us in our misery!' said Mr Donovan. 'Clinging to the rock in the rush of the towering waters, and giving up any hope of salvation. Picture my friend here, a man with a long seafaring life behind him, who has seen many marvels, but never one to equal this, when a boat is seen making towards us, and he cries out with tears streaming down his face, "For the Lord's sake – there's a lassie coming!"'

I blushed deeply. All I could remember were faces screaming in dumbshow, the words blown away on the wind, the fear that their panic would destroy us . . .

'So the lifeboat came out, but came too late?' said the younger reporter.

'Some twenty minutes later,' said Father. 'In coming out they did what we did not think possible . . .'

But Mr Smeddle cut into what he was saying. Mr Smeddle was most kindly smiling – I might almost say beaming – at me, keeping my colour high.

'What a brave girl you are,' he said. 'We thought

71

your father was alone, and so could do nothing, and we never thought of you! There'll be a silk gown in this for you, Grace, I shouldn't wonder.'

And then they were all departing. The flotilla of little boats that had brought them was embarking a gentleman or two; Mr Smeddle's cutter was taking the strangers on board. I had to go down with Mrs Dawson, holding her arm all the way and handing her into the boat. She looked around her, distraught and flinching at the sight of the waves dancing over the rocks and between the islands. A brave sight; but who could blame her?

The reporters had spoken so kindly to me, that I looked around for something to give them in answer to their words, but with such a run upon our stores there was next to nothing at hand, so I made presents to them of several parcels of dried fish, at which they smiled at each other, but I promised them they would have good eating. There were words of congratulation all around us, and promises – to Father that our stores would be made good, to my mother that coal tar and softsoap and polish would not be forgotten, and the borrowed clothes our guests were wearing would be returned to us when the Castle Trust had met their want of new ones. Each of the eight departing rescued – Mr Tulloch was remaining with us for the while – made a thankyou to me and to Father.

We stood on our tiny jetty and waved them away on the light afternoon breezes, and silence returned to us. Four of us, and Mr Tulloch, and a sudden space and quiet in our round rooms and comfortable kitchen. Mother looked round, and said to me in dismay, 'Oh Gracie, what a housekeeping is to do!' So we put on our burlap aprons, and rolled up our sleeves to the elbows, and set to.

Every bed in the house, every blanket and bolster cover; every inch of brass stair-rail, every tread of every stair; every pane of window glass, every flag of the kitchen floor, every chair-back, pan handle and door handle seemed greasy damp and finger-smirched. There were many days' cleaning and burnishing ahead of us, and not a tittle of the work of a normal day could be neglected. Most of the past few days went clean out of my head, and I made the most of that pleasure a woman has putting all to rights and apple-pie order. I did think about the silk dress.

I thought about the cutting scraps on Thomasin's floor. And about the little samples she had got from Macclesfield to show her customers. I think it was for Mrs Smeddle she had got samples of silk. And we had both liked a blue sample best, but Mrs Smeddle had chosen a red check on grey. I thought about that blue silk as I worked. My best dress is a pretty pink muslin, and I would rather have something different, were I to have another. The Macclesfield silks are 'shot' so that they catch the light this way and that in two colours, and the one I was fancying in my mind's eye was blue and grey – the colour of the sea in sunlight and of the sea under cloud both at once. I thought it might be trimmed very well with ribbons of indigo. Because my hair is brown, and my eyes dark, Thomasin would tell me, I knew, to have a brown silk for a gown; but I shall have that blue, I thought.

I did not stop to ask myself what I would be doing, that I would have occasion to wear such a dress – church on fine Sundays is the grandest outing we make ever – but I would have been pleased to have it, even so.

And I had no thought as I worked at washing our bed-linens, what was to happen to me. When the lighthouse was clean and bright again the thing was all over, I expected, and our life would resume its quietness and working days and nights. So that of all that happened afterwards I expected nothing; and the one thing I did expect – a blue gown of Macclesfield silk – I never did get it.

· 8 ·

On Tuesday, the morning after our survivors were all gone, save Mr Tulloch, Brooks went off to the main very early, saying he would come again at once if Father or Mr Tulloch were wanted, and bring them over to Balmboro', for we had understood Mr Smeddle to say the inquest on our first-found three dead would be held that same day, and Brooks was full of eagerness to see and hear it all. He did not return, and we were going quietly on with our washing and scrubbing, and Father and Tulloch were out upon the rocks with Father's gun, hoping we might have some wild duck for the pot that supper-time, when we were much surprised to see some people upon Harker Rock, beside the wreck.

Father and Tulloch rowed off at once to see what was about. He returned in about an hour with four gentlemen, to whom we served coffee and hasty cakes, this being all we had to hand. The newcomers introduced themselves as Mr Just, the manager of the Dundee shipping company, and a director, and they had with them two gentlemen being relatives of lost passengers. While we put their coffee before them in our best cups, Father and Tulloch were apologizing to them – 'I am sorry we broached you so abruptly, sir,' Father was saying, 'but Mr Sinclair put Tulloch here in charge of the wreck, and appointed me a deputy agent, and having no thought but that anyone properly concerned in the disaster would be in Balmboro' this afternoon, we thought you might be up to mischief.'

'Your watchfulness does you credit, sir,' the director said.

Mr Just said, 'Who is Mr Sinclair? And what business has he appointing agents?'

'Mr Sinclair is Lloyd's agent in Berwick; it is as deputy Lloyd's agent he has appointed me,' Father said, 'and he has requested Mr Tulloch to stay here and watch over the wreck.'

'Ah,' said Mr Just. 'Well, that was reasonable enough. I agree to that.'

'But what is all this?' said one of the other gentlemen. 'I don't understand . . .'

'It must seem very unimportant to you compared with the loss of your cousins,' said Mr Just quietly, 'but there's money at issue now. Lloyd's must pay up for the *Forfarshire*, and anything that remains of her is their property, you see.'

'Could you care for another cup, sir?' asked Mother.

'Forgive me, sirs; and you are welcome to as much coffee as you can drink – but are you not in a hurry?' said Father.

'Should we be?' said Mr Just.

'We were surprised to see you here at all,' said Father, 'for we thought the inquest was going forward this afternoon.'

'An *inquest*?' cried Mr Just, jumping up. 'So soon? Were there bodies found already?'

'There were three, taken from the wreck yesterday,' Father said.

'But we were in Balmboro' for over an hour, finding passage out here,' said Mr Just, 'and nobody mentioned an inquest to us!'

Father could not conceal his surprise, but he said, 'Our news is yesterday's. Perhaps we are mistaken.'

'I smell mischief!' cried Mr Just. 'Mischief and bad faith! Leave that coffee this instant — we are going at once!'

And they tumbled out of the lighthouse, and down the steps as though the devil were after them, and hoisted the sail of their boat so hastily we thought they would capsize her, and were gone.

'Well! and not so much as a thankyou to us!' said Mother, more astonished than angered.

'Other things to think on,' Father said.

'But perhaps the inquest is put back, Darling,' said Mr Tulloch. 'For surely they would call on both you and me to be witnesses?'

'One might think so,' said Father.

But it was not so; the inquest was indeed going forward while Father and Mr Tulloch shot duck, and Mr Just and his party inspected the remains of the wreck. Brooks came home late and greatly excited, and told us all about it.

Brooks told us there had been quite a pother. Mr Smeddle had run about — or ridden about, rather — all over the county, getting it set up. 'He was in a devil of a hurry,' Brooks said, 'and folk that I spoke

77

with could not make out why, but there it is, he would have no gainsaying it, but it had to be put in hand today.' Not that it was easy: first the coroner was away from home; somehow or other Mr Smeddle found a deputy coroner from Newcastle. Then there was some difficulty about where such a hearing could be held, since it seemed the castle was not thought suitable, and Mr Ross allowed the use of his house, though the jury had to be led through the length of the high street to view the bodies which were in a cellar at the castle, and back again to deliberate their finding.

So what with one thing and another, there was nobody who seemed to Brooks to know one end of England from the other as far as shipping was concerned. The coroner had called witnesses – he had called on the steerage passengers – two of those we had rescued. They had said they heard the Captain say the ship was due to have new boilers. The Captain had brought them some porter, for they were labouring at the pumps all night, and they had heard him say about the boilers.

And then Mr Donovan was called, Brooks said, with what we had all heard him saying, about how the ship was unseaworthy, and the boilers had needed to be put out before ever she left the Humber, and had he been the master, he said, he would have thought it his duty to put back into Hull . . .

'Yes, yes,' said Father, 'we have heard this song of his.'

Well, then, Brooks told us, the coroner told the jury that there were two of the company's directors in Balmboro' that very afternoon, who had not seen fit to present themselves . . .

'But, Brooks!' I cried. 'The gentlemen were here, and they knew nothing about any inquest!'

'Wait till you hear what happened, Gracie,' said Brooks. The coroner then said that was all the evidence they had available, Mrs Dawson being so distressed he would not call upon her unless the jury insisted; and so off the jury went into Mr Ross's upstairs parlour to think it all over.

'They didn't call anyone from the crew?' Father asked, shaking his head.

'Not a one,' said Brooks. 'And I forgot to tell you, Father, in the morning's bustle about, I detained Mr Smeddle a moment outside Thomasin's door, and asked him if he wouldn't want me to fetch over Mr Tulloch or yourself, and he tush-tushed me and said there was no need in the world and you both had a-plenty to do out here. Else I would have come for you, as I said.'

'There would have been no good coming for us if we weren't to be called,' said Mr Tulloch. 'But . . .'

'You haven't heard the best of it,' said Brooks, enjoying being the news-bringer. 'The jury was scarcely a few minutes gone out, when in comes the men from the company, wanting to be heard.' They didn't just want it, Brooks said, they demanded it. And they were told it was too late. 'They was absolutely fuming, Father,' said Brooks. 'I never saw a gentleman so angry as they was in all my born days, but coroner wouldn't mind them. He said they could stay and hear the verdict like everyone else. So they did, and this is what it was. I wrote it down for you so I'd be sure to get it word for word, for I knew you'd want to know it exact.' And he handed Father a paper from his pocket.

Father put up the paper close under the lamp and read it to us – '*Wrecked on board the* Forfarshire *steam packet by the imperfections of the boilers, and the culpable negligence of the Captain in not putting back to port.*'

'Neither true nor fair,' said Mr Tulloch, seeming much upset.

'What was said about the rescue, son?' Mother asked Brooks.

'Why, and that's another thing!' said Brooks. 'Nothing! Nothing while the inquest was sitting. No witness from the lifeboat, and none from the lighthouse! You'd have thought those bodies had swum ashore of their own selves for all that was said about it – not a word of thanks from that Smeddle for any of us, although he was so hot to have us go out and try it! There were reporters buzzing like flies round the rescued passengers,' he added, 'and they were blabbing on about Gracie and every word being written down.'

'Didn't you say anything yourself?' asked Father.

'Naw!' said Brooks grumpily, in his best Sunderland voice. 'I took myself down the road to Sunderland to sup a drink in sensible company, awa' from that mad-house!'

'I don't blame you, Brooks,' said Father, at which I looked up from my darning, for Father looks severely on the Ship, as a rule.

We were interested enough in all this at the time,

for so great an event as the wreck of the *Forfarshire* and all its consequences was in the forefront of our minds. But only on looking back do I see how that inquest was the thing that started all my troubles. The whole of England came to read about it. No doubt Mr Smeddle meant well. He was full of rage at the loss of life, rage at the crew who had saved themselves without thought of others, rage against any who might be to blame for the disaster. He chose his witnesses, whom to call and whom not to call, wanting to have no mention made of weather, and much ado made of faulty boilers and guilty owners; I am sure he did not mean to cry up my morning's work, and have the courage and the sufferings of the lifeboat crew overlooked; but whether he intended it or no, what he did had that result, and who can blame people in Sunderland for resenting it bitterly?

· 9 ·

When the great crowds of people came they seemed many of them surprised to find us what we were. And we for our part were surprised at their surprise. It is beyond me to understand them; what manner of people did they think to find upon a lighthouse? This is a lonely employment, being cut off from the mainland many days in every year, and detaining at least two members of the family to guard the light and its workings; and yet you must not think we were unused to company; in good weather we are nearer to Balmboro' than many of the Cheviot farmers are.

And we keep good company, too. We are more used to the company of gentlemen than many a farmer is, for some come to shoot birds, and some to observe them and to list them. We have many friends among the naturalists at Newcastle, in special, to whom Father sends reports of the migrations of the birds, and sightings of species which interest the Newcastle society from time to time, and for whom we stuff specimen birds taken here. It is Father's skill to stuff birds, and mine to find eggs, of which they also want a collection. I have to watch Brooks, who will make breakfast of a rare egg as gladly as of a common one.

Some of these learned men have been coming off to us, and lodging with us, for many years, like Mr Shields of Wooler, who paints birds, and likes to talk with Father. When first he came to us he thought of himself, I believe, as an explorer – one going to the North Pole, almost – and was charmed and amused to find our rooms warm and comfortable, and our food good. He was at once our friend. Mr Shields says this nineteenth century is a new age of discovery – but this time it is not new continents which are being revealed, but the world around us, and the creatures in it in all their wonderful variety. If we note something never before observed about the flight, or the plumage, or the breeding patterns of the sea-birds which surround us, he says we are a new kind of Columbus! It is true we watch closely the living creatures of the waters and the winds. There were no birds on the Longstone when first we moved here, and Father missed them, and put weed and soil upon the ledges to entice the nesting pairs, and now we have dirt-birds, and sea-parrots, and bell-ducks, their noise and their flight to watch from dawn till dusk.

Naturalists, though they are best liked here, are not our only visitors. For people are often curious about the working of the light, and when the weather is pleasant they will come from Balmboro' or Sunderland, or break the passage they are making to or from Holy Island to spend an hour here. And the Brethren of Trinity House may come at any moment to inspect our establishment, and have indeed come, more than once. So that though we have long lived on a remote rock, we were well used to the company of gentlemen. To those strangers who have had the effrontery to be surprised at our good manners, I would say: have they themselves, then, parleyed on equal terms with learned naturalists, as Father has? Did they think we would be unaware how to speak with any but mermaids and seamonsters?

Then again, it has been made matter for comment that my family is independent, capable and well read. Can you imagine! A fine thing indeed it would be to have people in charge of a lighthouse who were dependent on others for every little thing – or indeed for anything! What do they think would happen to such namby-pambies the first time storms cut them off from the main? And how would it do to have a man in charge of the lamps and machinery who could not read regulations, or keep records, or mend mechanisms when needful? My father is more independent by far than most men of his sort upon the mainland are; in these parts most men must defer to the Crewe Trustees, and if not to them, to the Duke in Alnwick Castle; my father is at the bidding of the Brethren of Trinity House. He has often told us that he who has two masters instead of one may largely please himself.

I have been stung to indignation by things said and thought about me; why should anyone suppose I would be ignorant? Everyone in my family can read and write. My brothers were at the school in Balmboro' Castle; and I went for a short while to a Dame School on the mainland, but I liked better to be at home, and so I have been brought up on the islands, learned to read and write by my parents, and knit, spin and sew. Our rooms are full of books; not a few belong to us, but we have the use of the free library in the castle as anyone in Balmboro' does, and except for novels we may borrow and read freely. Father will not have playing-cards in his house, for he holds them to be the devil's story books, and no novels either, which he thinks are but waste of time; but we have geography, history, voyages and travels with maps, so that Father can show us every part of the globe, and give us a description of the people, manners and customs, so it is our own blame if we be ignorant of either what is done, or what ought to be done. Why should anyone write to me, 'That you, ignorant of the ways of the world, should do such a thing . . .'?

At first, when the strangers began to come, when gifts and letters and honours began to be given me, I was pleased. A little abashed, but pleased, as I think we all were pleased at first.

Some five days after the inquest, a yacht from Lindisfarne brought us two young ladies and their brother, and it was quite a to-do getting the ladies ashore without wetting their silken hems. They were called Lukas, and were from Lancaster, but staying on Lindisfarne. Each Miss Lukas was picked up bodily by Mr Lukas and put down fairly dry upon the lighthouse steps, and they came in. And we were always pleased to see people; until then visitors always made a stir for us, and we were for the most part left to ourselves, for all that I have said about company. Until then Father or Brooks would take the visitors aloft to see the light, and Mother would put out a little to eat and drink, and I would keep about what I was doing. Father was very amused when he understood they had come to see me, and not the light, and he called me to them, laughing.

Hastily I put a clean apron on, and went down to them. Then they stared and blushed, and said nothing but, 'Oh, Miss Darling!'

'We are come to admire you, Miss Darling,' their brother said. 'My sisters would give me no peace till I brought them to look at you.'

'But —' said one of the blushing girls, 'you are quite pretty! You are quite small and ladylike!'

'Emily!' exclaimed the other, and then fell silent.

'We were expecting some kind of Amazon, Miss Darling,' said Mr Lukas, nudging his sister hard.

'Would you like to come up the stairs, and see from where I first saw the wreck?' I asked the young women. And the moment we were out of earshot of the men they lost their shyness and we talked together easily. I told them what had happened, and they plied me with questions, and we were well on the way to being friends, though some of their questions surprised me.

'What were you wearing, Miss Darling?' Emily Lukas asked me.

'Why, let me think — yes, this same dress I am wearing now.' Whereupon the other Miss Lukas, Eugenie, reached out her hand, and touched a fold of my skirt, to my great amazement.

'And on your head?'

'I had a bonnet on — to cover my curl-papers!' I said, and we laughed together pleasantly.

'I shouldn't think the poor creatures you rescued would have minded seeing your curl-papers,' said Emily.

'But I would have minded their seeing!' I said. 'I have a proper pride, you know, Miss Lukas.'

'Oh, of course you do! Why, Miss Darling, look at your lovely brown hair, your tiny hands, your slender wrists . . .'

She had me blushing violently now. '. . . We must have a memento of you; a scrap of your dress, a lock of your hair, a line of your handwriting – something – anything – indeed we must!'

I was very taken aback. I looked around my room for something to give them, but I do not have trifles and knick-knacks – or rather I did not then.

'My writing is not my best part,' I told them, 'and my dress will not grow again; you had best have a snippet of hair.' And looking in the mirror I pulled free the end of the plait of hair I wear coiled on the top of my head, and trimmed them a piece with my scissors.

Receiving it, Eugenie suddenly found her tongue. 'I wish I could tell you, Miss Darling, what you mean to us – your deed, so affecting, has given us hope; will be an inspiration to us for ever, for ever!'

'It was but my duty that I did, Miss Lukas,' I said, embarrassed at her fervour. 'As I am sure you would do yours on any occasion.'

'You have given us hope!' she continued, as though I had not spoken. 'A testimonial that the noblest feelings may inhere in a womanly bosom! That our sex is not for ever cut off from the possibility of heroic acts; that to be female is not always to be weak and helpless! You have reconciled us to our gender, Miss Darling, and we must thank you for it, however deeply you blush!'

'Why, and you prove one may be pretty as well as brave!' said Emily, laughing, and trying, I think, to speak more lightly, before all three of us were exhausted from blushing.

'Get along with you both!' I said, as though they had been my sisters, and with that we descended the stair to the kitchen, and Mother served tea, somewhat more mashed than perfect, because of the time we had taken aloft.

'You have been so long with my sisters, that you will not grudge me my turn to admire you, Miss Darling,' said Mr Lukas, as I handed the plate of bannocks to him.

I was blushing again. 'You are all most kind,' I said, turning away from his intent gaze, 'but there is no cause . . .'

'No cause?' he cried. 'Have you seen the newspapers?' And he took from his inside pocket a folded copy of a paper, and set it upon the table.

'No, we have not,' said Father. 'Does it report the inquest on the wreck?'

'Why it is about nothing else!' cried Mr Lukas. 'I must read to you from it!' and unfolding his paper he began to read aloud in a dramatic voice:

'And here it is our gratifying duty to record an effort made for the unfortunate sufferers by two individuals . . . whose heroism never was exceeded in

88

any similar case, and is of so extraordinary a character that had we not heard its truth attested by those who were benefited by it, we could not have been induced to give it our belief, ranking as it does, amongst the noblest instances of purely disinterested and philanthropic exertion in behalf of suffering individuals that ever reflected honour upon humanity.

'There! What do you think of that?'

'There are so many long words in it, sir, that I am not sure I understand it,' Mother said.

'Why, you will easily understand this,' Mr Lukas went on:

'. . . Darling is one of the two individuals who have so honourably distinguished themselves, the other being Grace Darling, his daughter, a young woman of twenty-two years of age! The latter prompted by an impulse of heroism which in a female transcends all praise, seeing that it would have done honour to the stoutest-hearted of the male sex, urged her father to go off in the boat at all risks, offering herself to take one oar if he would take the other!'

Mother beamed at him. 'This is really in the paper you are holding?' she said.

'Indeed it is — and it will not be in this paper only. The entire north is ringing with your family's praises, and the London papers will surely print the story. Your daughter will be the most famous young woman in England, except, of course, our dear young Queen. I will leave you the copy, ma'am; we can easily possess ourselves of another.'

'But it is not true . . .' I said. For surely, I had not really urged Father to take risks, had I?

'Why Gracie,' Father said to me now, 'of course it is true – indeed you did offer to take an oar.'

At that I was silent, for I couldn't deny that. And yet I was glad enough to see the back of our visitors, for being so stared at and spoken of had given me hen-flesh.

When they were gone, Father sat down with the paper, and read to us a good deal of it. It told over much that we already knew; it was full of condemnation of the crew of the steamer who had escaped leaving the passengers to drown. There was nothing in it about the lifeboat. But there was more about us, in the leading article of the paper:

We cannot close these remarks without alluding to the noble feelings, and heroic conduct of Grace Darling and her father, standing in bold relief as they do to the craven and unseamanlike desertion of a part of the crew. The humanity and fortitude of those two respectable individuals is beyond all praise, and cannot fail to bring down upon them warm thanks and blessings, if not more substantial marks of approbation.

'There!' said Father triumphantly to Mother, as he finished. 'And you would have had us not go, I think!'

'It is good to see a little praise for Gracie,' Mother said. 'She is a good girl, even if she doesn't sew as neat as Thomasin.'

'Does a substantial mark of approbation mean a silk dress, Father?' I asked him.

'It might!' he said, laughing. 'It might!'

· *10* ·

Before September was over we were beset with artists. And they came with letters from friends in Newcastle, from Mr Hancock and others whom we would hate to disoblige, or with commissions from Mr Smeddle. I did protest to Father, that I had very little time to sit still and be painted, let alone time to sit in the coble, and seem to hold an oar, and put on over and over again the dress and bonnet and shawl that I had worn that melancholy morning, while the rooms were still to be kept neatened, and the work of house and light was still to do, and he replied that Brooks should help me clean and ready the lights. Brooks was rather more at home than he had been; he loved company, and now there was plenty of it, for not only were the artists staying with us, but there were divers working on the wreck, and it was but a short row for Brooks to join them, and assist, and bring away bits and pieces. Of course, the larger part of what was salvaged was sold at auction, and raised five hundred pound; the bits and pieces Brooks brought us were one or two dinner plates, with a picture of the vessel on each — for she had had her own fine dinner service for the saloon, just as Mr Donovan had related — and a piece of marble from a broken fire-mantel which Father worked into an inkstand. Brooks was interested in the diving; and besides, he was uneasy in Sunderland, these days.

The first of many artists to visit us were Mr Watson and Mr Dunbar. Mr Dunbar had come to take likenesses of Father and of me for marble busts, and he came with letters from Mr Smeddle, and brought his friend Mr Watson with him. We had seen some marble effigies of Mr Dunbar's in Balmboro' Church – and until then I would have thought, I admit, that only the dead ever had their faces done in marble. But Mr Dunbar intended hundreds of copies of his handiwork to be made in plaster for sale to the public. He was not very long about the work; perhaps that is why it did not much look like me, but I did not care, for I thought what I look like is my own business.

We discovered in Father an admiration for artists, which a little surprised me, until I reflected what pleasure we had from the pictures in his beloved books of histories and travels; to my complaint he answered that it had so fallen out that we were able to help honest workers in pencil and paint to earn a little money, and it would be churlish not to help them; besides, we would share in the profits from their work, by and by.

'How so, Father?' I asked. I could not imagine he would charge a price to be painted.

'They have all said they will make a donation to the fund,' Father said.

'To what fund, Father?'

'Why girl, the fund talked about in the papers!'

'I have not had time to read papers, Father.'

'See, then,' he said, and showed me a pile of papers which he had kept in his cupboard. He made me sit down and read, and I learned that in Newcastle, and in Durham, and in Edinburgh, there had been meetings, and speeches about the *Forfarshire*, and subscriptions had been opened to reward the Sunderland boatmen, and Father and me. The reports of the meetings spoke of Father and me in most extravagant words. They were like the stares of the Misses Lukas; they gave me hen-flesh.

But when I once got used to the steady staring of a painter at work, there was some pleasure in it. Being painted allows one to stand still, and be quiet, and think. Of course the artists who drew and painted me made pleasant conversation; but long silences fell between us as they worked. I have been very little used to standing still. At first my fingers twitched to be working, for I never sit down but I pick up some sewing or knitting, and I asked Mr Watson particularly if I might not knit while sitting for him. But he told me no; I should keep looking down at my needles, and he needed to see me stock-still, and looking level at him. And soon I found that such stillness brought a new feeling to me – a reversal of the way I most often felt. My days would often leave me very tired in body, and fretful, and underworked in my mind. This is why reading is such a refreshment and a relief to me, why Father has always thought I was the one of his daughters who could be contented in the life on the Longstone. But sitting many hours together, unable even to sew, rested my limbs, and gave my mind freedom to wander.

I thought on pleasant things, and of fair-weather days in my recollection, and that was delightful to me. But there were other thoughts to trouble me. I recollected often of the wreck of the *Forfarshire* – of the terrible moments when the bulk of the ship sank full of helpless living souls to the bottom, and of the distress of those who had stood in the fury of the blast, waiting for dawn. The dead gentleman who had perished of cold before we reached the survivors was a man of God, a Reverend Robb, and all Balmboro' was full of pity for his family and friends, whose grief had been most touching at his funeral, and whose report of the poor dead man was eloquent of his virtues. A better and kinder man never lived, we learned. I could not but wonder why such a one should have perished, and others been preserved by Providence to be rescued by Father and me. Or indeed, why on a night of such fury, such a taking of souls, Father and I should have been spared from sharing the general disaster, and permitted by Providence our safe accomplishment of rescue.

That the hand of Providence was more accountable than the shipping company seemed now very clear – for a second inquest had been held on the first of October, with the regular coroner in charge, and this time it had heard evidence for the company offered by Mr Just. Mr Donovan was still in the neighbourhood, lodged by the castle, and he had repeated the stories he had told to the first inquest, but this time he had been questioned, and contradicted himself, and the second verdict when delivered found that the body was that of a person 'wrecked upon the *Forfarshire* in consequence of tempestuous weather'. That verdict was good news to Father, for he thought it fairer; except to the Sunderland boatmen, that is, for once more they had not been mentioned.

Mr Watson stayed a few days longer than Mr Dunbar, though they had come together, and besides painting he went fishing and fowling with Brooks and Father, and became quite a friend. He was a humorous, light-hearted young man, who had me laughing a good deal, and got on famously well with Brooks. Brooks rowed him to see what remained of the wreck, and somehow, getting him upon the rock contrived to have him tear his trousers.

'He was so tremendously embarrassed at it,' Brooks told us, 'that I tried to comfort him by saying that after all there was none to see save myself. And he answered that there were millions of gulls!' Brooks was scarce able to tell us, for laughing, 'and one in particular, that he was sure was staring with a beady eye upon the revealing gash in his garment!'

Mr Watson might indeed have been such a one as to be embarrassed by a gull, for he could not bring himself to mention his trousers when it came to asking me to mend them for him, but colouring deeply he requested a little sewing up of a gash in his 'Inexpressibles'.

We were all very merry together over that. We were laughing till the last moment he was with us, for when he took his leave he said to me very solemnly that his admiration for me was inexpressible – and I asked him if in that case it needed mending, and if so in which leg!

But there was more than laughter in being painted by John Reay. He came to us unannounced, though bringing letters from Newcastle friends, on the first fine morning after a three-day storm. The storm was severe, though not as bad as the one which had destroyed the *Forfarshire*, and we had water into the kitchen. We had opened the door and swept the water out, and though it was chilly at mid-morning we had the door standing wide to admit sunlight and air and dry off the damp flagstones of the floor, and we saw William Swann's boat tossing on the swell, and bringing a stranger huddled in his cloak.

The stranger, when unwrapped in the kitchen, was a young man of delicate appearance, and golden hair, who was trembling from head to foot. We hastened to close the door on the boisterous wind, and put a chair by the fire, and Father offered him a sip of whisky to steady him.

'This een's freet o' the sea, and has had a hard time coming out,' said William Swann, accepting a courtesy tot of the whisky, and sitting himself at the table. 'But ye'll not blame him when ye know . . .'

Looking round the room, and his eyes lighting on me, Mr Reay said to me in a shaking voice, 'Oh, Miss Darling, you have saved my life!'

'Not I, sir,' I said to him.

'You have, in a way, Miss Grace,' said William Swann.

'But what can you mean?' I said, now mightily astonished; I already expected nonsense in the mouths of gentlemen, but William Swann is a boat-man!

'Mr Reay got off the *Northern Yacht* in Sunderland, in order for to paint you, Grace; and she passed by Lindisfarne, but never got to Leith, her next port of call. She's been searched for when the storm dropped down a bit, but it seems certain she is lost, with all hands.'

'I too intended to go to Leith,' said Mr Reay. 'But hearing of your famous deed I changed my mind, and broke the journey, hoping you would consent to be painted. Had it not been for you, you see . . .'

When Mother and I saw that the newcomer meant it, and that he was much upset, we made a pot of tea, and warmed a plate of bannocks, and set out a dish of jam, and bustled to make him welcome, and comfort him the only way we knew. We are not likely to make light of the tremors brought on by a narrow escape; we know them in our own flesh. Meanwhile Father and William Swann were talking at the table, and I half overhearing them as I helped Mother.

'I have a letter from Trinity Brethren,' said Swann, putting it on the table. Father seemed surprised.

'I have reported to them already,' he said.

'We have not been rewarded yet, Darling,' Swann said. 'And there is fear that we shall be forgotten. All the talk and all the writing in the papers is about Grace. And some about you.'

'Mr Smeddle told me there would be a distribution of reward,' said Father. 'And are there not funds being collected for us all?'

'People are saying perhaps you have taken your share and left us to fend for ourselves.'

'We have not had a penny piece yet. And I have given my word to try to see fair dealing.'

'Well, that's what I've been telling people,' said Swann. 'But the sooner it's paid the easier I'll feel. We had a hard time over that.'

'Indeed you did. We all know that.'

'To read the papers you would think . . .'

'What can anyone do about the papers?' Father asked. The question went unanswered.

I am soft-hearted, Brooks tells me, a perfect fool when anyone has need of comfort, even to a sore finger, or torn inexpressibles. When a handsome and gentlemanly stranger seems distressed and in need of comfort, even if I thought the distress somewhat fanciful, how could I not warm to him, gentle him, try to steady and to cheer his frightened thoughts? Mr Reay was both excited and terrified by his close call with death; and though we mocked him gently – comparing his safe disembarking at Sunderland from a ship then whole, with the terrible trials of our most recent guests, torn from safety by the rushing waters and rending timbers of the ship, and cast out on to remote rocks in the fury of the storm, this tactic did little for him. It only made him shudder the more, speak with the more horror and loathing of shipwreck and the implacable seas, express even more admiration for what Father and I had done, and even more emphatically assert that I had saved his life!

He babbled on in this fashion all the evening, and ate very little food at dinner, to Mother's deep concern; all's well in the world for Mother as long as everyone under her roof has a hearty appetite! But the next morning he rose early, and very cheerful, and began to unpack his paints, and ask me to put on what I had been wearing that fateful morning.

'No dressing up for vanity, mind,' he said. 'I want this to be exact.'

'Then you must wait while I put in my curl-papers,' I told him. His face fell, so that I laughed at him.

'Shall we settle for exactness in everything but the curl-papers?' he said, smiling.

'Will you be long?' I asked.

'Not above three days, if you stand still.'

'Three *days*! How am I to find such leisure as that? I have work to do, sir. You must make do with an hour or so at a time.'

'Very well, that will be pleasant enough. I shall contemplate the sea and the wild birds, and wait for you to come again.'

He made me stand, holding a loop of rope, and facing the light from the northern window, and he set to work.

I let my thoughts fly free, but they came back swiftly from blue silk dresses, and a Christmas present for my little nephew Billy, to the Sunderland boat, and the premiums they were looking to receive. Surely they were entitled to the bounty for

99

the first boat putting out to a wreck; they must have put out before us, since having come much further they reached the rock so soon after we did; they must have been due the bounty for bringing in a body . . .

By and by, 'You are looking troubled, Miss Darling,' he said to me. 'Please to look bonnier.'

'Why, would you have people suppose that I rowed out in a tempest looking cheerful and unconcerned?' I asked him.

'But I do not paint you rowing; I paint you standing safe at home, the object of general admiration.'

'The admiration is very silly,' I said. 'And fast becoming tiresome. I would you would show me as I am, and no better.'

'Showing you as you are will not diminish the admiration by a tittle, I fear,' he said, looking at me very intently. I felt myself blushing a little.

'I am inundated with letters, and have very little time to answer them,' I told him. 'Besides, I scarcely know how they should be answered. What am I to say to the lady whose letter arrived with you yesterday, who has sent me a five-pound note, and asks for a lock of my hair?'

'You might send her one. Where's the harm?'

'Why, if I send one to everyone who asks, I will soon be as bald as a coot!' I said. 'And besides, to be candid, the thought of it gives me hen-flesh. I had never thought to have given away a lock of my hair, except to a sweetheart.'

'I find suddenly a most intense desire to possess a small lock of your hair, Miss Darling,' he said. 'Will you oblige me? I am afraid I am but a poor artist, and I cannot offer you five pounds!'

'Did you not hear what I said?' I asked, half laughing, half vexed.

'Oh, I heard you,' he said. 'That is why I want it so badly.' Then when I refused to answer him, only shaking my head, he said gravely, 'I need it for a colour sample, to make perfect my painting of your bonny brown hair.' He looked at me so earnestly that I think I almost believed him; enough, anyway, to uncoil my plaited bun, and clip him a piece from the end, with the little scissors that I keep handy tied to my apron band. I found a scrap of ribbon to tie it tight, and gave it him. Then while I stood, twisting my hair into place again, and pinning it there, he, looking at me all the while, kissed the lock of hair, and put it in his upper waistcoat pocket, against his heart.

'Fie on you, sir!' I said. 'Think you not shame to beguile a young woman so?' And he had beguiled me, for in my secret thoughts I was pleased.

'I had need to beguile you,' he said, smiling. 'When I asked you straight you said no. And now this shall comfort me in the long hours of night, when the morning I so desire is slow in coming. If only you knew with what joy I awake to a day in which I am to paint you, to look at and talk to you . . .'

I myself would be glad of every hour of sleep I could get, for I would be working long past my bedtime, to make good the lost hours spent in so pleasant a way, but I said to him only, 'But tomorrow you cannot paint me, you know, for I am to go to Balmboro' Castle. Mr Smeddle has summoned me. He has something to give me, he says. Saburn will bring a boat over at nine.'

'We must on no account disappoint Mr Smeddle,' said he. 'Mr Smeddle is to exhibit paintings and drawings of you and your father in the castle, and I am hoping to sell my work then. I shall wait on your return with brush poised and ready.'

'But really I cannot sit for you tomorrow. When I get home there will be the day's work to do.'

'Let me do your tasks for you while you are gone,' he said smiling.

I thought of the scrubbing and the cleaning of brass and carbon-black, and lenses and window-glass, of the washing and ironing and making ready of wildfowl and rabbits and a pot-bunch of carrots and turnips . . . 'You are not able, sir,' I told him.

Mr Smeddle kept us longer than we had thought at the castle. He received us not in his little office, where usually folk who had dealings with him were received, but in the castle hall. I had never been in so grand an apartment in my life before; it was high-roofed like a church, and lined with panelling and decked with old weapons and paintings in gold frames. In the middle stood a table of immense length, and in a huge hearth a bright fire was burning, though it was yet early in the day. Mr Smeddle was standing with his back to the fire; but my eye was drawn at once to a stranger sitting at the table, who was very finely dressed like a man of rank, but of a complexion somewhat weathered.

Mr Smeddle bade us sit down, and I did. Father remained standing, his seaman's cap in his hand, turning it by tiny degrees round and round as he stood.

'This is Mr Blackburn,' Mr Smeddle told us. 'He is come from the Duke of Northumberland at Alnwick, expressly to see you. What do you think of that?'

Truth is, I was terrified at the thought that the Duke had so much as heard of us, leave alone sent a fine gentleman to meet with us. 'I am much surprised, sir,' I said.

'Come, Smeddle, no need for that,' said Mr Blackburn. 'My dear young lady, I suppose you know that England is ringing with your praises from one end to the other? Here on the board between us' – he pointed to three leather boxes on the table – 'are three silver medals, entrusted to myself and Mr Smeddle to be conveyed to you; and Mr Smeddle has also, I think – have you not, Smeddle? – a number of presents to you from members of the public.'

He opened the boxes in turn, and we all inspected the medals. Three bright discs of silver, crisply minted, lying in red velvet, and strung on red ribbons were displayed. The Glasgow Humane Society, the Leith Humane Society and the Edinburgh Humane Society had each given me their medals for saving of life. I had never till that moment heard of any of these societies. Of course I felt pride to have been given their medals. Mr Blackburn asked us for an account of the rescue, that he might make report of it to the Duke, and so we told him what had happened as best we could. Father explained most carefully that we had discussed together what might be done. 'We agreed that if we could reach the rock,' he said, 'there might be some there who were strong enough to help us row back.'

'And had the poor sufferers been too weak, when you reached them, to assist you?' Mr Blackburn asked.

'We had no thought but that we would then share their fate,' Father said. 'We did not think the lifeboat from Sunderland could reach the scene.'

'And you, Miss Darling? You were ready to try this chance, thinking it might cost you your life?'

'My daughter said she would have tried it alone, had it been needful,' Father said.

'These medals have seldom been so well deserved, if ever,' said Mr Blackburn, giving them into my hands. 'And now I have more to tell you. There have been meetings to raise subscriptions for you in many towns and cities; even in London, I hear. There will be money enough to set you up very comfortably in your rank in life. Several hundred pounds, at the least. What do you say to that?'

'People are very kind,' I said. 'It is not needful. But I am grateful for such kindness. Sir, I hope that everyone who shared in the danger that morning will share in the subscription . . .'

'The Duke is very fair, Miss Darling. Very fair. You may rely on him for that.'

We took our leave, and Mr Smeddle walked with us to the castle gate, as though we had been grand visitors. He had a number of parcels to give us, and many letters.

'Mr Smeddle,' Father said to him. 'May I speak my mind, sir?'

'Of course, of course, Darling. Speak to me as you would to a friend.'

'All this talk of money, Mr Smeddle. I will be very glad to see something done for my daughter. But with us it is not a hard case. I am well able to see to my family's needs, and it is no matter to us if something which is promised to us is not paid for many months. But with the boatmen, sir, it is a different matter. They live from hand to mouth, and must often eat bread and broth in a house where the larder is bare. They may be hungry whenever storms keep them from the fishing. And Thomas Cuthbertson scathed his leg in getting the boat over the Longstone rocks, and it has not healed. He is kept from working. There will be ill-feeling, sir, if their courage is not acknowledged. And there is no knowing, Mr Smeddle, when next there may be occasion to wish for a lifeboat to put out to a vessel in distress.'

Mr Smeddle heard him out. 'I thank you for the warning, Darling,' he said. 'I will see to it at once.'

To me he said, 'Thank you, Miss Darling, for signing the cards I sent you. They have given pleasure to many of my friends. I hope you will not mind signing some more? They are in one of the letters I have given you. At your earliest convenience, please sign and return them to me.'

Saburn was waiting for us on the beach. There was a light breeze offshore, and his boat sped away, her sail swelling, running directly towards the Inner

Ferne, where we called on Mr Smith, the lightkeeper there, with some messages and stores. Father and Mr Smith talked a little. Mr Smith had got some salvage from the wreck, which was to dispose of, and Father wished to know if Trinity House had written to him, as they had to Father. I walked upon the little beach below the lighthouse and the buildings, searching for shells, as I had done when a child. I found nothing special but a little space of quietness to be myself in, and a tiny pink shell with a pearly lining.

'What is this about signing cards?' Father asked me, as we made the passage onwards, past the Brownsman.

'It seems people want a line of my handwriting, and Mr Smeddle has promised it to them. And look, Father, here is a note from Thomasin, asking the same thing!'

'I can see nothing wrong with that,' Father said. 'Only foolishness. A little kindness, and you may give them what they wish.'

'Father, this will be nearly a hundred cards for Mr Smeddle!' I said. 'And I don't know how many letters to be answered, and here we are going home cumbered heavily with more, and with presents too. I must write letters half the day to keep kind and mannerly towards all these people; and I must sit still half the day to be painted by artists, and there was little enough time to spare in the day before ever this uproar started . . . and truly, I scarce know which way to turn!'

'Well, then, we must do what we can to help you, Gracie,' he said.

We were passing the Brownsman, then, and Saburn put in to let us gather some potatoes and leeks, which we did in but a few minutes, and then we went on, under the Pinnacles, like castle battlements, all white with the droppings of the wheeling and screaming sea-birds, in all their variety of kinds, auks, and guillemots and terns and kittiwakes, oyster-catchers, eider ducks and shags; then we were round the corner, and the Longstone rose up before us. The tide was near its highest, and the rocks of our island at their smallest visible, and little white waves were dancing all over the water. The seals on the rocks looked at us with sea-deep eyes, and the horizon lay beyond, broken only by the sails of a passing ship. The cares of the mainland fell away from my shoulders as I came home to the tower steps. Out here the mighty weight of Balmboro' Castle was but tiny, scarcely visible on the distant shore.

Before we went in, Father said, 'Take heart, Gracie; the fuss will soon die down, and we shall be left alone to live our lives in quietness again.'

We handed the medals round to be looked at by all before dinner; and the stew for dinner was welcome and good, though not quite as good as usual, because Mr Reay had insisted on helping Mother ready the pot-posy of vegetables, and he had left a good deal of the skin on the carrots and turnips! He was very pleased with himself, notwithstanding; 'You see, Miss Grace!' he said. 'I promised to perform your duties while you were gone!' We were laughing at him, and with him, when he picked up one of the medals. It was struck with a picture of a man being drawn by two seamen naked from the water into a boat. The words were 'Let Not the Deep Swallow Me Up'. Seeing it, Mr Reay grew suddenly serious, and said to me, 'I shall never forget it. You saved my life.'

· 11 ·

Father woke me at the end of his watch; mine was the morning watch, always, from four till putting down the light at dawn. He had a lamp in his hand, and as I rose and put on my gown he lingered at the stair head. I saw he had a paper in his other hand.

'Will you look this over for me, Gracie?' he said. 'I want no mistake about it.'

'What is it, Father?' I said, rubbing my eyes from the sluggishness of waking.

'The Trinity Brethren have asked me for a second report upon the *Forfarshire*. This is my reply to them.'

I held the paper in the pool of lamplight, and read it where Father's finger directed:

At about one quarter before five, my daughter observed a vessel upon Harker Rock; but owing to the darkness and spray going over her we could not observe any person on the wreck, although the glass was incessantly applied, until near seven o'clock, when, the tide being fallen, we observed three or four men upon the rock. We agreed that if we could get to them some of them would be able to assist us back, without which we could not return; and having no

*idea of a possibility of a boat coming from North
Sunderland, we immediately launched our boat . . .*

*Afterwards the boat from North Sunderland
arrived . . . and came to the Longstone, with great
difficulty and had to lodge in the barracks three days
and three nights with scant provisions, no beds, nor
clothes to change them with . . .*

'This is precisely your recollection, Gracie?' Father
asked me.

'Yes, Father. Why have they asked you to state it
twice?'

'My first report was too brief, it seems. This one
had better be careful.'

'It is in every particular correct, Father. Why does
it worry you?'

'Only that it be correct,' he said. 'I harkened what
you said about the work you have to do, Gracie, and
I have asked Thomasin to come off for a week and
assist you. She has a dress to finish, but she will
come tomorrow. And I have found you this.'

He handed me a book of advice on the writing of
letters, with examples for every occasion. I thanked
him, hugging him. Then I went up to check that the
light was turning smoothly, and watch for the rise
of day.

It was a clear dawn, still and calm. And I had just
extinguished the flame when I heard a light step on
the stair. It was Mr Reay who appeared to join me.

'What are you doing so early, Grace?' he asked.

'My morning's work,' I told him.

'I shall not hinder you. I shall watch you,' he said.

I did not much relish being watched by a gentle-man while I rolled up my sleeves and got sooty to the elbow cleaning colly-black off the reflectors, and I doubted he had the patience to watch for long.

'See, then,' I told him, 'I have snuffed the flames, and trimmed the wick. Next I must scan the horizon, and then clean the glass and copper.'

'I shall help you scan the horizon,' he said. 'That is my kind of work.'

'It is not your kind of work at all!' I answered. 'We must record any shipping in sight; the type of vessel, and if we recognize it, the name, and the course it is setting.'

'And are you not allowed to contemplate the beauty of the morning? You have a set of vistas here that would shame the prospects from the windows of the greatest lords on land. Are you not sensible of the beauty which surrounds you?'

'Of course I am sensible of it! I love my home very dearly, and can never bear to be away from it for long. And I observe it every morning of my life.'

'Tell me then, what is the light like this morn-ing?'

'Bright.'

'And?'

'Bright and clear.'

'Bright and clear, and of what hue?'

'It is the colour of buttercups,' I said, after thinking for a moment.

'And over there – that swelling mountain that I can see far behind the shoreline – what is that?'

'The Cheviot.'

'And what colour is the Cheviot, Grace?'

'Blue, from here.'

'Blue? And what colour do you say the sky is, and the sea?'

'Blue,' I said stubbornly.

'Were I to paint everything blue we should not be able to tell one part of the picture from another,' he said. 'Wait here a moment.'

He descended to his room and came back with a cup of water, and his box of colours. 'Look,' he said. 'For the Cheviot on this radiant morning I would start like this with a brushful of indigo . . .' He twirled his wet brush against a block of paint, and put a sweep of colour on the white lining of the box lid. '. . . and then add crimson, very little . . .' He looked hard at the distant shore, and dabbled a little red into his colour, and looked again and added a little more, and then a little more blue, until his pool of colour matched the shade of the distant mountain, softened by the haze, standing bravely in the morning light. 'Now what colour do we have?' he asked me. I shook my head. 'What flower might I paint with this?' he demanded.

'Violets? Or if it were lightened a little, lilac?'

'Clever girl. What colour should I mix into it if I wished now to depict the underside of that line of cloud that hangs above it?'

'You would need some grey, I think.'

'And to get grey I would start with a smidgeon of black . . . there is nothing wrong with your eyes, Grace, only with your habit of looking. Here I have better than two dozen colours in my box, and not one would ever be right for a piece of the real world without mixing! Now tell me carefully what we can see all round us.'

'Eastward an empty horizon, and the rising sun,' I said. 'You would need . . .' I looked in his box, which he held open to my view, '. . . citron yellow; but moments ago it was nearer chrome.'

'Wonderful!' he said. 'Go on.'

'Turning north, that line of . . . indigo . . . is the promontory of Holy Island, Lindisferne, with its ruined castle on the rising bluff; westwards the whole line of the shore, in shades of lilac, and violet and blue, and nearer to us the other Fernes; that green-topped isle the Brownsman, and to paint our sometime cottage and lighthouse tower you would need . . .' I looked again, 'sienna in this morning light, but later, perhaps, umber. And white for the lighthouse on the Inner Ferne. And chrome and umber mixed for the line of the shore, where we see that narrow streak that is the wide sands, below the castle and church. You might do those in the same colours as the Brownsman buildings . . . No, they are so much faded by more distance you will need your lilac brush again . . . Then to the south, that distant promontory is Dunstanboro' – where you can just see the jutting ruin stand at midday against the light. It is scarcely visible now.'

'Picture yourself Dunstanboro' at midday. What colours shall I need?'

'It is blacker with brighter light behind it. And I am very sure you will not have, nor can ever mix a colour to catch the brilliant sparkles on the sea in a light southerly air!'

He laughed, his face bright with pleasure. 'I am only an artist,' he said. 'Not the Deity himself!'

'I knew that, sir,' I said, and before I turned, reluctantly, to my dirty job of burnishing, I added, 'It is always a wonder to me, how from the land the Fernes seem cast far out to sea; but from here the land seems to curve round us, and we contained in a bay of great beauty. Do you not think so?'

'Yes. Beauty everywhere one looks, here,' he said, looking at me. But then to my relief he had done, and went down, and I could get my task done, and scrub my hands before readying the breakfast and waking my parents.

I had need to sit – or stand still, rather – for Mr Reay, for the better part of three days more. Thomasin was doing my work all this while, and her own sewing was waiting till the evening. None of us had seen the picture that was in the making, for Mr Reay would not have it, but kept his easel covered over. The letters I had brought from the castle were lying unopened and unread upon my writing-desk, and each day William Swann came off with more. By and by I asked Mr Reay why he need take so long.

'I am working as slowly as I well can, Miss Darling,' he said to me. 'But I cannot help it but I will be finished by tonight.'

'But how inconsiderate of you, sir, to spin it out longer than need be, when I am so busy, and leaving all go by the board!' I cried. 'I believe I will go at once, and start about my own affairs, and you can finish without me!'

'Don't be hard on me,' he said. 'Cannot you see to what state your comeliness has brought me?'

I coloured, and did not answer him; I did not know what to say.

'Beauty of face and form has never yet deprived my nights of rest,' he said. 'Beautiful women are commonplace enough to an artist like myself. But beauty of soul; beauty that does not know itself, and puts on no airs, and partnered by a man's courage, and a man's dignity! You have no equal, Grace, in the wide world beyond your lonely tower, of which you know so little! Come with me; let me show you the world!'

'You know I could do no such thing!' I said indignantly.

'As my wife, you could.'

'I do not think to marry, Mr Reay,' I told him.

'Why not? You will have wealth and fame, and may do as you please. We will go first to London, and then abroad. You can have no idea of what treasures the world is full; you shall hear fine music, and see palaces and pictures, and talk to interesting people every day of your life ... In me you would have a husband who owes you his life, and well knows how to value you; who would never reproach you with your northern voice, your work-toughened hands . . .'

'You must see, Mr Reay, that I have spent the whole of my life in the care of a father who is a model of his sex. Who is strong and capable and knows well what to do. I could never entrust myself to anyone whom I less respected than I do him.'

'My dear Grace,' he said to me, 'I will not be offended by those words. But in them I see clearly what you do not see; how very little of the world you know. No doubt but that your father is everything that his station in life requires of him, and that on the Longstone I am but a fool, a cack-hand at every job. But in my world on the wide mainland the matter would be reversed; you would see me at ease and respected, and your father nonplussed; there are many kinds of men, Grace, and therefore more than one way of being an excellent fellow.'

'I have yet to see my father nonplussed.'

'I see that I have offended you. I did not mean to. By and by as you are dragged into the public eye, you will understand what I mean.'

'I think any husband of mine would have to live upon the Longstone. And I do not mean to change my name, and submit myself to governance. Any husband of mine should take my name for his, instead of the other way about!'

'Well then, my dear, you have refused an offer of most true, most deeply felt love,' he said. 'If ever you change your mind, you must write to me, and I will come at once and carry you away to the nearest altar, and beyond, to the glories of the world, and I shall be the happiest of men. Tell me at least that I may hope for it.'

'I promise you that if ever I change my mind I will write for you to come for me,' I said. 'But do not hope for it.'

'Hope is not readily forbiddable,' he said. 'Do you want to see your picture?'

He had drawn me looking thoughtful, soft; but not a fair likeness. He made me oval-faced and pretty, and he had left the neckscarf off my attire, showing my neck and collar-bones in the neckline of the dress.

'You have made me look like the Queen!' I said. 'I have a more jutting chin than that.'

'I do but put down on paper what I see,' he said. 'Never forget me, Grace.'

We all stood upon the lighthouse steps to wave goodbye to him, when he left. Brooks was taking him over, in a flat calm, to Sunderland. As soon as he drew out of earshot, Father said to me, 'Well, Gracie, what answer does he have?'

'What do you mean, Father?' I asked, astonished.

'Why girl, he asked me if he might offer you marriage. Did he not do so?'

'Yes, he did, but I did not know that you knew of it. What did you say to him, Father?'

'That I hardly thought it suitable, but that he might try what you would say. What did you say, girl?'

'I said him no, Father.'

'I am glad of it,' Father said. We went back into the kitchen, and closed the door.

'You were not fond of such a wisp of a man, Gracie?' Mother asked me.

'I was not; but I would like Father to tell me what was unsuitable about him,' I said.

Father sat down in his chair, and took up his

whittling knife. 'He has no money for a wife in his way of life,' Father said. 'I thought perhaps he might have smelt a whiff of money about Grace, what with talk of funds and subscriptions. Perhaps I wrong him, but as it falls out it is no matter.'

That night when Thomasin and I lay down together, she in my bed, and I in the truckle bed beside her, she said to me softly, 'He was unco' handsome, Gracie, though, thought you not?'

'Oh yes,' I said. 'And kind, I think.'

'You were not hankering to look after him for life, though?'

'No, truly not!' I told her.

I did think a little of John Reay, of his fair hair, his smile which dimpled one cheek only, his gallant manners and appealing words. It was in the night watch before dawn that I had time for my thoughts to wander. And they did wander away from time to time with the lock of my hair that he had tucked in his weskit pocket; but when my thoughts ran that way they did not touch the place where deeper yet in my memory was kept an image of Thomas Cuthbertson, handing me smiling into a boat, and saying, 'Lass, thou's mayed to my fancy!' Or wedged in a corner of roofless wall, his face turned up to the pitiless beating of the tempest, and the rain on his cheeks like tears.

· 12 ·

When Brooks came back from taking John Reay to the mainland, he came with news and letters, and two more painters. So that there had not yet been a single day since the wreck which we had had to go about our lives to ourselves. These latest comers were Mr Parker and Mr Carmichael, and so eager were they to see the few spars remaining of the *Forfarshire*, and the very place where she had struck, that Mr Tulloch got up from his chair – by now it was his usual chair – in the kitchen, and rowed them to Harker to see it before the light failed.

This gave us space to hear news, and open the letters. 'The Trustees at Balmboro' have paid the boatmen five pounds,' Brooks said.

'I am glad of it,' Father said.

'You should rather be sorry than glad, Father, for it is not enough,' said Brooks. 'What – five pounds between six of us?'

'It is not generous, considering what was suffered,' Father said. 'But it is five times the regular bounty for the first boat to put out to a wreck.'

'But open that letter, Father, from the Trinity House Brethren. Everyone in Sunderland seems to know what is in it.'

Father took up his penknife, and carefully slit open the letter. It contained money. Two bank notes in the order of ten pounds, as the letter said, a free bounty for Father, and another for me, for our courage and sense.

'This is the rub,' Brooks said. 'Five between them; and twenty for the father and daughter? I have left my share on the table, so that at least the others may have a round sum apiece.'

'You did well, son, and I will put that right at once,' said Father, taking a sovereign from his box, and giving it to Brooks.

'Oh, Father, it isn't the money in my pocket!' cried Brooks. 'It is the misery I am in among my friends!'

'Let us have this talked straight between us, Brooks,' Father said, sitting down, and pointing to a chair for me, and one for Brooks. Once we three sat down to the table to talk it seemed grave enough. 'We all know there's competition to save and salvage, and scavenge and fish. There's a natural grief when anyone strives for advantage and fails. But in my mind, *they* did what *I* didn't think possible – they got here – and *we* did what *they* didn't think possible – we got there with only the two of us, and one being Gracie. Who got there first was chance, if it wasn't Providence. Any one of the Sunderland boatmen knows that. They won't be grumbling long over twenty pounds.'

'Oh, but it's much worse, Father! There's talk of vast fortunes for Gracie; of money pouring into subscriptions from all over the country – it's in the papers every day! They are saying the Queen in London has sent fifty pounds! They are saying Gracie did nothing at all; that the people rescued themselves by walking over here at low tide; that there was no danger at all – the rocks giving lee – all sorts of spiteful talking. They harp on about Harker Rock not being in Darling territory, but in theirs. They are laughing and jeering at the words in the papers which say 'without hope of reward . . .' and saying they know better, and it was all from greed, and snatching the bounty from under the noses of the lifeboat, they are saying it cannot have been much, else a girl could never have done it . . .'

'Hold hard, boy,' Father said. 'Territories are agreed for fishing, and for salvage, not for human life. When it's life in the balance that comes before anything. As for what was done – you and your bullies saw what the state of the wind and water was that day. Whatever may be said, the boatmen know well what was done, and whether it was worth rewarding.'

'But by so much, Father! So much for Gracie, and so relatively little for anyone else!'

'And beaten to it by a girl!' said Father bitterly. 'That's what stings, no doubt of it! But think on it, Brooks; even had we thought it probable that the lifeboat would get out from the main, should we have stood by watching while people stood naked to the wind, and wet to the skin, and bone-cold, and frozen, and simply waited for the boat? What if others had died while we waited? My conscience is clear on the matter towards any man. Now, as I understand it, the funds being raised are for everyone; doesn't it say "For the Darlings and the Sunderland boatmen"?' Father stabbed at a newspaper column with his finger. 'As for the share-out, that won't be down to us. The gentry will settle that over our heads, being our betters, and we will take what we're given and say thankyou.'

'But will they deal fairly, Father?' said Brooks. 'For if not, I tell you, Gracie will be in a fair way to be hated at home as much as she's admired everywhere else!'

'Fair?' said Father. 'Will the gentry deal fair by our way of thinking? Most likely not, Brooks, and there's nothing in the world we can do about it. Just look at the state of things, son. In my father's memory, and almost within mine, a wreck was seen as fair game for poor folk. Poor folk were half starving, and would pray for a shipwreck! I can call to mind people praying, not quite that a boat might be wrecked, but that if God was minded to wreck one he would cast it up right near them, where they might feel the benefit. Not surprising if the gentry didn't like it; but gentry with common sense could see that you couldn't expect a poor man not to help himself to property floating free on the tide; and you couldn't expect a man with children to feed to risk his life for nothing. That's what the premiums are for; that's why the Crewe Trustees pay them as well as keeping lookouts, firing guns, giving relief to the shipwrecked. That's why the Trinity Brethren have paid us this, that's why there's a lighthouse here in the first place. We are all being paid, Brooks, to be rescuers rather than wreckers. Only having set up a system to pay poor men to risk their lives, they don't like to think the money enters into it at all. They like to fancy that it's all done from high-mindedness. There's some of them would be shocked rigid to think anyone might think of rewards when someone is drowning. Especially if a gentleman was drowning; mark me, Brooks, if that boat that got clear of the *Forfarshire* had been found full of passengers, and not a man of the crew in it, there wouldn't have been a stink about that! But a life is a life to my way of thinking.

'I do believe Mr Smeddle will make sure that there's some kind of rough justice, because he knows it'll be awkward the next time if he doesn't. We'll all get what we had any good reason to expect, otherwise, they think so little of common folk, they would fear to be back with wreckers again. Though to my way of thinking, it doesn't come down to money, but to whether you've got the stomach for the job. It's a naked instinct to save a fellow creature if you can, but it takes mettle. You know that well, my son. As for the fortunes being talked of, *if* they come to us, that's because people are moonstruck over Gracie. They think it's marvellous a young woman could do what she did. Well, I think so too. Whatever she gets, she deserves it. A man couldn't have a pluckier daughter, even if she was a son.'

'I'm second to none in thinking well of Gracie, Father,' said Brooks.

'And of yourself, Brooks. Keep your own head high. But I'll not miss a turn in trying to keep your part of the story to the forward. What else can we do?'

The neither one of them asked me what I thought about it, and the parley was broken up when back came Mr Tulloch in the coble with our two new painters.

Mr Parker and Mr Carmichael were friends, and had come together to make a terrific painting of the rescue. Mr Carmichael said he was an expert at 'seascapes', a word which gave us much diversion together, for we took it at first to mean escapes at sea. Then of course we gave him various words of our own for 'seascapes' in his meaning – seaglim, sea glower – and we translated our name 'Glororum', as in Glororum Shoal, to them, for it means 'Glower o'er em . . .' or a place from which one may see a distance. They both being Newcastle men, they could talk to us in northern fashion, and were interested in our island words. Mr Parker, on the other hand, was good at painting figures, and at shipping. Between them they thought to produce a famous masterpiece, or so they said.

I was not pleased to see them. John Reay's going had left me with a strange kind of hollow feeling, and it oppressed me as I hastened yet again to clear a room, and make up fresh beds for the newcomers. It was with little grace that I thought of more time spent standing or play-acting mock-rowing the coble, while the day's visitors thronged around – for there had begun to be visitors every day of feasible calm – and on my desk the threatening pile of letters and parcels grew higher and higher.

But there was no resisting Mr Parker's kindness. His young wife was expecting a child shortly, and he spoke of her with such affection and concern, and used such gentleness with me, as would have melted away any reluctance from the hardest heart. And this tribute I must make to Mr Parker, that of all the thousands of strangers who have stared and ogled at me now, he alone could stare at me and bring me neither blushes nor hen-flesh. I learned at once, as he began to look at me and draw, that there was a way of looking at my face to see the line, a way of looking to guide the eye, which such as he might use upon the fold of a dress, the cloud in the sky, the tilt of a spar, the form of a rock, or, if that happened to be the matter in hand, the shape of a woman's face; a way of looking which had nothing to do with a man looking at a woman, and which could leave me unassaulted, unembarrassed. I saw at once in the contrast how John Reay had not for one minute of his long hours working looked at me like that. And soon I learned also from Mr Parker that John Reay was not the cleverest artist. In Mr Parker's drawings I did not look like the Queen, nor like a beauty, but much like myself.

And strangely, I felt more flattered by the plain likeness than I had by the flattering one.

But it was not because of his superior skill that we thought so well of Mr Henry Parker. He had a pleasantness with us all. He had come to paint the rescue; but he sketched Mother, too. He talked with Father and Carmichael, and went rowing about looking at the lie of the land, or of the rocks and waters rather, just as Mr Watson had, but he plied Brooks with questions, and was quickly fast friends with him. He did not pick me out for undue attention as so many others have done, but took us as we are, a family, like other families, although our home is a tower, and our garden is the changing sea.

After nightfall the first day they two had been with us, we were sitting tight and cosy in the kitchen, with a bit of a wind and some rain beating at the windows, and a good rabbit pie inside us, and Brooks mentioned the lifeboat having come out. Mr Carmichael said he had some impression they had set out, but been forced to put back into safety – was it not so? – and so we gave our two visitors the full story, Brooks eagerly talking. When we got to the point of the tale where the bullies marched out of the lighthouse, Brooks said simply that there had been no room.

'What are these barracks?' said Mr Parker.

'They are a roofless corner of wall left standing,' Father told him. 'All that the sea has spared of the lodging put up for the masons when the tower was built.'

'I must see them!' cried Mr Parker, standing up.

'I will be glad to show you when the weather abates,' said Brooks.

'No!' said Mr Parker. 'Show me now, when I may get the feel of it. Will you come, Carmichael?'

'Oh, if you say so,' said Mr Carmichael, rising reluctantly from his chair.

Brooks took a lantern, and led them out, and they were gone some time, and came back, rather damp, in high excitement.

'Three days and nights of that, in desperate weather!' cried Mr Parker. 'I should have gone mad. Even thinking of it one might go mad!'

'There's some who find it easy to forget,' said Brooks sourly. 'But if Gracie had stuck to a woman's work, we should all be famous by now.'

I withdrew to my bed leaving them talking, for I must rise early, and was tired by such thronged and busy days. But I think a good deal was confided in our new friends, how we felt, how we feared to be blamed for injustice that was none of our making, for by breakfast of the next day Mr Parker announced that he and Carmichael would do all that they could to assist us.

'I have already started, as you know,' he said, 'a painting of this very kitchen, with you, Miss Grace, and you, Darling, bringing in the rescued, assisting them. I shall paint another, very like it, but with different figures. This second canvas I shall entitle, "The Darlings supplying refreshment to Brooks and the Lifeboat Crew". And,' he finished triumphantly, 'it is this second canvas that shall be exhibited in London! There! What do you think of my plan?'

We thought it wonderful, and very kind of him, and we helped him and Mr Carmichael all we could, and parted the very best of friends, with Father offering to recover for Mr Parker some piece of the timbers of the *Forfarshire* as a memento, and Mr Parker promising me, as he took his leave, that if his child was a girl it should be called Grace, and be my god-daughter, which promised me joy, and has indeed given me joy. I have been glad to find shells, and thread beads, and make dresses for little Gracie, for in such small favours I feel I am myself again. And she at least does not crave endless letters, and snips of my dresses and snips of my hair.

Letters! I do not know how many letters I have had to answer. And how am I to answer? How to answer a consignment of a silver mug for Father, with his initials, and the date of the wreck upon it; a silver cream jug, inscribed 'For the mother of Grace Darling'; six silver spoons for me, and a Bible, richly bound and inscribed: *'To the brave-hearted girl who thought not of her own life while assisting to save the lives of others, this book is presented by some of her admirers residing in Smeeton near Nottingham.'* This with two letters, full of kindness. But also, I discern, as I sit down to make answer, full of grief. These people have lost a beloved friend, and it is this that has made them act so feelingly towards me.

I looked to Father's style-book for advice on writing letters.

Dear Madam,
I owe the receipt of yours of the 2nd instant . . .
which has been delivered to me by Robert Smeddle
Esquire of Balmboro' Castle; and in reply I am
requested by my dear father and mother to thank
you, also those other ladies and gentlemen
individually for their kind presents; for myself dear
Madam, I am quite at a loss in which way to return
to you a suitable answer.

The style-book suggested various expressions of delight on receiving presents, but I do not feel easy expressing delight, when the occasion of the present is the death of many. I must try to find words of my own which will fit the need better:

> *Had your valuable present not been associated with such a melancholy occurrence I might have said that I am delighted with it – but I must beg leave to say that the awful loss of human life caused by the loss of the Forfarshire debars me of that pleasure.*
>
> *Believe me, I sincerely feel for the loss you have sustained, but I trust your loss will be your friend's eternal gain . . .*
> *I have the honour to remain, dear Madam,*
> *Your very humble servant,*
>
> *Grace Horsley Darling.*

This alone took me over an hour to pen, and it did not, I thought, sound entirely right. Father's book gave an example of those lines about yours of the . . . inst . . . but I did not feel comfortable writing in such a way. And that one was easy! How I squirmed to discover that I had been so slow – so it seemed to them – in thanking the friends of Kirkaldy for a gift of a Bible, that they wrote again, inquiring if I had received it. I had, but among so many other things I had left it lying. I made excuse that the parcel had been tardy reaching me, and gave what thanks I could.

> *May our Almighty Preserver grant all my friends here with me the sanctified use of that Blessed Volume . . .*

That phrase I could copy from Father's book, which has advice on giving thanks for a Bible; but there is nothing in it about shipwrecks, so I must needs find my own words to finish −

> . . . at present everything that brings the awful scene to my remembrance leaves a degree of sorrow and regret that it was not in our power to do more . . .

but the style-book helped me end off −

> I remain, Sir, your very most Obt. Hl. Servant,
>   G. H. Darling.

And as well as letters, gifts! A golden locket, an inscribed silver cup, left at Balmboro' Castle by Lord FitzClarence, and the Earl of Errol − lads alive! how does one start a letter to an Earl? A gold ring set with amethysts, a dress ring, another golden locket, a paisley shawl, a silk mantle which I have not had, and never will have, an occasion to wear, a beaver hat lined with silk, the like of which is to be sold up and down the land called 'The Darling Hat'.

And every gift needed a letter. I will not say that the gifts were all unwelcome; I greatly liked the paisley shawl, and the gift of a workbox was very welcome to me − not even Thomasin had a nicer one.

And it is easy to write when really pleased!

> Dear Lady,
> I received your kind present of a handsome workbox from Mr R. Smeddle that afternoon you left Balmboro' Castle, and beg to return my most grateful acknowledgements for the same; the usefulness of such an article can only be judged by people like

myself who have had three or four places to search
when a little job was to do. I feel quite delighted
when anything is to do now, and an addition would
be added if you would be pleased to accept a lock of my
hair as a memorandum of
Your ever obliged humble servant,

G. H. Darling.

Should I have offered a lock of my hair in such a case? Perhaps it was not modest of me! But of course I wanted to make some small return of kindness. Nothing of all these gifts could ever be given away again, for fear of causing offence, and of my own otherwise I had so little, and nothing that could be spared. I might have made a little pincushion as a token of thanks, but I had not the time. And if my hair seems worth the giving, I have been taught to think so . . .

But if I was often at a loss to answer the letters coming showering in upon me, the worst of all were those containing money. Those put me in such a fright that Father helped me with them. After supper, night after night, when we had been used to be quiet together, with the light put up, and bedtime still a little time away, the time we had used for reading, or sewing or knitting, now was taken up with letters. I spread them on the table, and Father looked at them, and then, with his carving in his hands – he was making an inkstand for Lord Panmure out of a chunk of marble mantelpiece from the *Forfarshire*, the second such he had made – he dictated what I was to say about the money, and I added a few words of my own to each one:

Kind Sir,
I am very much obliged to the gentlemen who have
given me the sum of twenty pound, and I hope you
will let them know that I feel very grateful to them,
and I thank God who enabled me to do so much. I
thought it a duty, as no other assistance could be had,
but I still feel sorry I could do no more.

'That's very well, Gracie,' Father said. 'Now write: "Please, sir, I will thank you to pay the money into Messrs Ridley's at Alnwick, in my name." And sign it.'

I wrote as he directed. But I said, 'Father, is it quite right to take money from strangers?'

'Well, girl, how could we refuse it? Think for a moment — could we refuse without rudeness? I see nothing wrong with it. You will have what I never thought you would have — a nice little establishment of your own, better than I could have set you up, by far, and the thought gives me great satisfaction.'

'I thought I was always to be here, with you and Mother. I never thought of a life on my own. How would you do without me?'

'Well, there's two things to be said to that, my dear. First, if Brooks weds a sensible female and brings her offshore, he may become assistant, and hope for keeper after me, and his wife will have a pair of hands, no doubt. And then there's a great difference, Gracie, between having you here because needs must, and having you here because you choose to stay. I've found great satisfaction in this life, and I am pleased if you do too; you are a comfort to me, and a friend. But it doesn't fret me a whit to think you have the means to live otherwise if you like. Don't let it fret you.'

'If we were only as we were, Father, I could wish for no better life. But when every day brings all these visitors . . .'

'It'll die down, by and by,' Father said. 'Trust me for it.'

· 13 ·

Only in storms did we now have calm days. Every fair or half-way day the boats came out from Sunderland and Balmboro', bringing folk flocking like gulls. They came to talk and stare, and try to touch me, and talk nonsense, and ask questions. How they wearied me! At least while the painters were with us the visitors were restrained, and could only watch, and move on. But when we were alone they were everywhere about us, looking at our rooms, picking up things and putting them back, and giving me hen-flesh once an hour all day long.

How could I not go henny-fleshy, at the request of a man and his niece, from St Petersburg in Russia. They brought me gifts – a pair of embroidered slippers, and a silver girdle, which they called a cestus, and which might do very well in Russia, for all I know. But when the gifts were given, and my thanks returned, the gentleman brought from his pocket a miniature painting of his nephew, and requested me to kiss it. He was charged, he said, to make sure that when I had kissed it, it should not be touched again until the owner received it back. How heartily I wished I had the courage to refuse! And yet the thing was so stupid it seemed not worth the refusing at the cost of grave discourtesy to the gentle-man standing before me.

Worse – it stings me yet – was the poor High-lander who came calling on us in kilt and plaid, and was shown the tower, the light, the rocks – there was very little left of the wreck to mark the spot by then, but the waves had taken off the greater part – he, with tears in his eyes, told me he had nothing else to give but the silver buckle on his plaid, and taking it off he pressed it into my hands. He was, I think, honest in his words; I would have fervently refused to take from him the only thing of worth he had, which has lain heavy on my heart that I had it ever since, but that looking anxiously at his fevered expression I perceived just in time that a better kind-ness would be to take it. I used it at once to fasten my paisley shawl, and wore it till the boat carried him away again, and then I sat down quietly and wept in pure fury at people's folly, and my broken peace.

When Mother found me weeping she scolded me, and fussed me, and made me a cup of tea, and told Father, and I was forced to confess how tired I was, how my limbs seemed weighed down, and how for the first time in my life I dreaded each need to climb the stairs. Then Father gave Brooks my morning watch, that I might sleep a little longer.

I suppose I would have said all this was bad enough, but worse was about to come. My feelings were so bitterly mortified over Mr Batty's Circus that I can never recollect the matter without pain; yet still I scarcely know what I did wrong. Mr Batty sent us a copy of a newspaper, in which was a notice about his circus in Edinburgh, offering a sight of foreign horses, wild zebras, the royal elephant, vaulters, Swiss acrobats, fine horsemen, and suchlike. This came to us together with another paper, announcing that the proceeds of the performance on the 8th November would be 'For the benefit of Grace Darling'.

We were by now well used to hearing about subscriptions in our name – as well used as we were to hearing tales about giants and bogles from our childhoods, I sometimes thought. But we found pictures of wild zebras and elephants in some of Father's books, and took a little time amusing ourselves with the thought of such splendid creatures in Edinburgh.

On the eleventh Saburn brought out to the lighthouse a Mr Silvester, when we were expecting no visitors, and indeed, had none other, the weather being somewhat rough. Mr Silvester arrived looking a little pale from the pitching of Saburn's boat, but recovered quickly on getting a tot of Father's whisky, and introduced himself as Mr Batty's manager, charged with the duty of delivering a clear twenty pounds, 'Into Grace Darling's hands'.

There were twenty golden sovereigns, gleaming upon the table. 'It is not much,' said Mr Silvester, 'but it comes, dear Miss Darling, with the heartfelt approbation and I might say, love, of the people of the fair city of Edinburgh.'

I gave him thanks: 'I am touched, sir. How kind people are. You must not call this generosity not much,' I said.

'All I meant to say was that it is not much compared to the huge sums subscribed for you in the funds we read about in the papers,' he said.

'We have had private presents, in personal letters,' Father said, 'but for all that we have heard talked of, this is the first money from public subscription we have yet received.' Then the talk went quickly from the money to a question of whether I might visit Edinburgh, and see the zebras and the elephants, and the wonderful foreign horses. Mr Silvester said that the public which had supported the subscription would be overjoyed to see me, that I might have a ringside seat, and visit the animals in their cages before the entertainment, that Mr Batty would make every arrangement for my comfort, that Thomasin should come with me, or Father might, if he could get leave of absence . . . I looked anxiously at Father.

'Might I go, Father?' I asked him.

'If you would like to, Gracie, why not?' he said, and to Mr Silvester he said, 'My daughter, sir, has very little recreation in our way of life. And she has always been keenly interested in birds that are the only part of nature that can be studied here. Zebras and elephants would be a capital treat for her!'

I was much astonished, truth to tell, for Father is so set against plays and theatres – I had thought a circus might come under the same sort of cloud. I think it was the creatures of God's creation that made the difference. That very moment I sat down to write a letter to Mr Batty, that Mr Silvester might take away with him.

He particularly asked that I should acknowledge

137

the money; it was scandalous, he said, that other funds had not reached us yet, and he would be glad of a written proof of the honesty and dispatch with which Edinburgh's twenty pounds had been delivered. At Father's dictation I wrote that. And then with a beating heart, and full of excitement, I wrote, '. . . it having been intimated to me that my presence in Edinburgh would greatly oblige those who have manifested so much anxiety for my welfare, I will take an opportunity shortly of visiting your arena in person.'

Mr Silvester thanked me, drank tea, thanked Mother, was shown round the light, thanked Father, and went off again, to survive the rough crossing back as best he might.

It was from Mr Smeddle that we learned what happened next. My letter to Mr Batty was published in the *Mercury*, and then the *Edinburgh Observer* wrote a harsh article attacking those who had raised funds for us, with more than a suggestion that money was misappropriated. Mr Smeddle summoned us to the castle, and showed us the printed words in copies of the papers. He was most upset, and wanting to know how such a thing could have been written.

'This is not right,' Father said. 'We did not say we had received no presents. Grace has had a five-pound note in offer for a lock of her hair, and numerous other such. But it is true that of the large sums mentioned in the papers as subscribed for us by the public we have had nothing, nor any precise reports. It is true, but we did not ask Mr Silvester to print it. I should have consulted with you first, sir, before desiring any such thing.'

'Yes, yes, of course you would,' said Mr Smeddle, seeming mollified. 'It is just these rascally journalists who rake up scandal when there is none, and get good people like yourselves into trouble.'

'Are we in trouble?' Father said. 'Of what kind?'

'None that I cannot deal with for you,' said Mr Smeddle. 'Sit down, sit down, and we will talk. First, as to funds, the money is in the hands of very eminent persons. The highest in the land, in many cases. Naturally it is unfortunate that anyone should imply that it will not reach you. But you yourself, I am sure, would wish it to be carefully reflected upon, and most fairly divided between all concerned. That will take time.'

'Mr Smeddle,' said Father, 'I would have you understand us. We are not asking for money to be paid to us for doing what we took to be our duty before God. But it cannot but damage my daughter if the whole world thinks she is wealthy, while in truth she has little or nothing. I am sure that you must see that, sir.'

'I see that perfectly. And I will explain all this to the Duke. I will take pains to explain it. I will make sure that he knows the newspaper article was none of yours, so that you may stand in his good favour as securely as before.'

'The Duke?' said Father, blanching a little.

'Did you not know that it was he who is supervising the funds?' said Mr Smeddle. 'Everything is in his hands. That is what makes this newspaper article so impertinent! But have no fear, Darling; I shall assure His Grace that you are both very well behaved and deserving persons in your private capacity, and that the great sympathy shown to you by the public will not excite any feelings in you other than gratitude.'

There were then more presents and letters to be collected, which had been sent to Mr Smeddle for safe-keeping.

'All this is a tax upon your time, sir,' Father said.

'Not at all, not at all. Least I can do,' said Mr Smeddle. 'But if Miss Darling, while she is here, would be so kind as to autograph some cards for me, I would be most obliged . . .'

I wrote my name forty times before we were sent down to the housekeeper's room for some tea.

I hardly need say that we were mortified that our conduct should need defending to a Duke. But there was worse yet, far worse. I opened a letter dated Edinburgh, 14th Nov., and if I expected it would be praise, or overpraise of me, well, every letter preceding it had been so, and I read:

Having observed in the public papers that Miss Darling is about to visit the city for the purpose of exhibiting her person *in a* low circus of Mountebanks *if this be true (which we sincerely hope is not the case), we would with the utmost sincerity of friendship and admiration of her high character recommend her not to accept any such offer, as we are convinced that such a presumptuous step would bring a stain upon those unfading laurels which she has so honourably gained; a* stain *which could never be effaced . . .*

It was unsigned. I stood trembling, not knowing what I thought at such a shock, and in a daze I went on opening the letters that lay before me.

Dear girl, the best of womankind, how nobly your conduct incites your sex to the performance of good deeds . . .

that was another like the usual ones. But then:

The Ladies who are conducting a subscription in Edinburgh for a testimonial to Grace Darling have been led to do so from a belief that it was in a humble dependence on the protection of God that she was led to act . . . from so noble a motive . . . the greatest injury has already been done to the well-earned reputation of Grace Darling . . . therefore it is the earnest hope of those who are now interesting themselves . . . that she will refrain from an exhibition which has already made a considerable change in the sentiments of those who were desirous to befriend her.

Dry-eyed, and shaking, I took these letters to Father. They made him white with rage. He stormed out of the house, and spent an hour chopping driftwood violently with his great axe. I would have liked to break plates, if we had any spare. I knelt on the hearth at Mother's knees, and put my arms round her and wept into her apron. She stroked my hair, and by and by she sang to me, as though I had still been a little child:

Aa-you-aa my bonny bairn,

Aa-you-aa upon my arm,
Aa-you-aa thou suen may lairn
To say Dadda, sae canny . . .

When Father came in again he was calm enough. 'Unsigned,' he said, picking up the letters and casting them into the stove. 'Malice and wickedness always goes unsigned. Forget it, girl.'

'But, Father – others may go to a circus! Why may not I?'

'I don't know,' he said. 'Did these fine ladies think you were to put on pink hose, and dance among the acrobats? I don't know; only, Gracie, I think now you had best stay home.'

'Oh indeed I shall!' I said. 'I couldn't bear to go, now!'

You may imagine what a short answer was got by the manager of the Adelphi Theatre in London, offering me fifty pounds plus all my expenses, to sit upon the stage in a cardboard boat and pretend to row; or to the man who wrote to Father in the same bundle of letters, 'I am of opinion that if she were brought out in proper style in London as an exhibition, that much would be done for her good.' This last writer seemed to think that Father might come along with me to protect me. How he supposed the light-house would go along meanwhile, we had no inkling.

The fuss about Mr Batty was still not over, though the letters were burned, for Thomasin came off the next morning, quite unexpected and very agitated, bringing a copy of the *Edinburgh Courier*, which one of her customers had shown her.

We read with sinking hearts:

We believe all parties are agreed that the conduct of Miss Darling in saving the lives of the crew of the Forfarshire *was the brightest example of heroism devoted to the cause of humanity that has been exhibited in modern times. Those who admire that conduct will be the first to deprecate the conduct which has since been pursued towards her, of dragging her before the public on all occasions, and for the most trifling causes. That Miss Darling should submit to this can excite no surprise. Born, we believe, and certainly brought up on a rock in the middle of the ocean, and from that cause as ignorant of the world as childhood itself, it is not to be wondered at that she should submit, without contempt and indignation, to the meddling interference of those who, under the pretence of gratifying her are only intent on ministering to their own vanity. The letter we have quoted confirms us in this opinion. It is clear that she has no conception of the nature of what she there proposes to do . . .*

We were all at sixes and sevens reading this. Thomasin thought it had been printed in the papers that I would perform in a circus; Mother thought it was defending me, saying clearly that I had not known what I was thinking to do; and I – how could I not be angry on being defended by the assertion that I was but an ignorant child?

Father said, 'This has gone far enough. I shall see to it,' and he put on his hat and coat, and asked Thomasin to stay off, for he would be gone overnight, and he took the boat back that was waiting for her.

We had a little peace together then, as we used to long ago, when she lived here, and we two had George and Brooks in charge. We found a piece of pretty sprig-muslin, and cut out a dress for me to make for Mrs Parker's expected baby. Thomasin showed me a new hem-stitch she had learned, and we were quiet together.

Father came back the next day at around five of the afternoon, bringing Brooks with him. Father had ridden all the way to Berwick, and stood in the editor's office of the *Courier*, and demanded that they print a correction. He had refused to go home till such was printed, and the editor had entertained him to several pints of porter while they waited, and let him see the printing-presses at work, which had much interested him. He put down on the table before us a copy of the paper, and then he took off his coat, and sat down and read it to us.

'*We last week stated on the authority of a letter inserted in the Edinburgh papers, that this young lady had acceded to the invitation of Mr Batty to visit his arena in Edinburgh; we now allude to the subject to give it unqualified contradiction. Miss Darling has no such intention, her present popularity is without her courting and she will take no means of intruding on the public notice.*

'There,' he said. 'That will be that, I think.'

'Thank your father, Grace,' Mother said. 'This errand has taken the last of his three nights a year permitted to him to be away.'

Of course I thanked Father. And Brooks shortly had us laughing with a story of how being in Alnwick on some errand he had thought to get his hair cut, and have a shave. And while he was in the barber's chair a hawker had come in with a tray full of tresses, selling them at a shilling a time as being Grace Darling's.

'I leapt out of my chair with the foam all over my face,' Brooks told us, 'and I overset his tray and chased him half down the street, with people all staring and cheering. They were none of our Gracie's – why they weren't even her colour, but sandy!'

Even so, 'I won't leave you sad, Grace; I'll stay another night,' said Thomasin.

'Do, do; but I'm not sad, dearest,' I said.

Sadness was not the name of it; nor was I in fright, but rather in the fear of fright – for had not Father thought I might go to the circus? I was stung by the word ignorant that had been applied to me, but it was not that which troubled me – but what if Father himself, having spent his life on a rock in the ocean, were ignorant? What was it Mr Reay had said, about how it would be if Father were on the mainland? What if after all Father did not necessarily know what ought to be done? I began to know how it might feel to be embarked in a vessel whose captain had lost the mastery of her, which was rudderless in wind and waves . . .

Because Father had used his three nights' leave of absence, he had to write to the Brethren for permission to go with me to the Duke of Northumberland's castle at Alnwick. We were invited on gold-lettered papers to visit the Duchess, and receive from her fifty pounds from the Queen herself. And I was more alarmed at the prospect than ever I was at getting into a coble in rough water; the waves move in a fashion that I understand, having lived among them. I had thought to live and die and never see a Duchess!

Of course the leave of absence was at once given. The Duchess sent a coach to pick us up at the quay at Sunderland, and I was in some anxiety what to wear. I looked at the silk mantle, and the silver scarf I had been given, but it seemed to me not right to put on such finery. For although the Duchess was a grand lady, I was not, and I had no desire to seem to wish to be one. I had little time to give to such fretting, so that morning I put on a simple gingham gown that Thomasin had made for me, and the new paisley shawl I had been given, rejecting the Highlander's silver buckle for a plain pin of Whitby jet of my grandmother's to fix it by. I wore the beaver bonnet from the hatters' society, which was plain enough, and needful in the sharp December weather. Father, of course, put on his Trinity House uniform, in which he looks finely his own man.

And I was glad I had not decked myself out when William Swann landed us at Sunderland. The coach had not got down the steep so far as the harbour, but was waiting for us at the top of the rise, and so we walked the quays and half a street in the morning bustle of the fishing-boats making ready to go out, with all eyes upon us. They were not as friendly to me as of old; I do not like to think what effect I might have had in a silk mantle and a silver cestus!

Alnwick Castle is in the midst of Alnwick town; my Lord Duke has a park, but it is behind the castle, not all around it. Alnwick has a gate astride the street, left over from the old town walls, and some fine streets of elegant houses, some wide, some close and narrow. I have visited there before, although not often, and we have a cousin there, and his family, John and Ann MacFarlane, who keep a little greengrocer's shop. You go up a narrow street and find yourself crossing into a wider one, and just round to your right suddenly you come upon the castle gate, standing up at the end of the street as though it were one of the houses. It is very dark-looking and ancient. Behind railings like those of a gentleman's house it looks somewhat like a toy castle, and there are statues set upon the top of it, just the way George used to set his toy soldiers when he was tiny. And although I knew of course we were going to the castle, I was surprised when the coach did not stop at the gate, but rattled us straight through it to a view of the massive building inside.

The coach door was opened as soon as it stopped by Mr Blackburn, who had come to see me at Balmboro'. He introduced himself to Father as the Duke's lawyer and factotum, and said he was sent to bring us to the Duchess. I did not at first comprehend what he could mean – for were we not just arrived? – but when I saw through what a maze he led us, I was glad of his kindness in guiding us.

I have a confused memory of courts, stairs, corridors, fine furnishings and paintings, and woven hangings, Chinese jars and bowls, but we were swept past everything at a smart pace, our footfalls ringing on fine marble floors, then muffled in patterned carpets. I had enough time to reflect how far above Balmboro' Castle these glories seemed, and then Mr Blackburn knocked upon a great door, and without waiting for answer opened it and led us in.

A very haughty-looking lady was sitting in a silken chair, most gorgeously dressed, and surrounded by light and pretty things – an embroidered firescreen before a fire in a white marble fireplace – pictures of hunting-scenes in faded flowery forests – I had but a fleeting impression, for I hardly dared raise my eyes. Mr Blackburn presented us, and withdrew, though I wished he would stay for already he seemed a friend, and the Duchess struck terror into my heart.

But I was wrong to fear her. She rose from her chair, and held out a hand to me; and spoke to me very kindly, and most courteously to Father.

She made us sit down, and she had from Father an account of the circumstances of the rescue, and then she turned to me.

'And when you are not rescuing seamen, Miss Darling, what is your favourite occupation?'

'The work of the lighthouse leaves me little leisure,' I told her. 'But I am fond of reading; and I have made a collection of shells.'

'The Queen will be very glad to hear it,' said the Duchess, at which I looked up astonished. 'You know that I was governess to the Queen when she was the Princess Victoria? She and I made a collection of minerals, which gave us much delight, and helped us pass many long hours. It is presently displayed in a tower here at Alnwick Castle; Mr Blackburn shall show it you before you leave.'

'Thank you, your Grace,' I said.

'It is enough to call me ma'm, my dear,' she said, continuing, 'the Queen has been wondering what sort of a girl you might be; I shall be pleased to be able to tell her you are a collector. Do you sew? Your sister, I am told, is a dressmaker.'

'I can sew, ma'm, but not half as well as Thomasin. I am afraid one may sometimes see daylight through a seam of mine if it is pulled!'

She laughed, and smiled at me. 'I can do nothing useful at all,' she said, gesturing with an expression of contempt at a workframe of fine embroidery that was lying beside her on the couch.

'Now, my dear young lady, do I understand that the public enthusiasm is becoming troublesome to you?'

149

But before I could answer, the Duke burst into the room. A great tall man in pale trousers and fine linen, he flung back the door, and bounded the paces needed to bring him over the plains of carpet to the centre of the room.

'I am amazed, my dear!' he said to the Duchess, who had risen, leading us to do so also. I thought perhaps she looked a little less than pleased, but the expression vanished in a moment. 'Here I am in my library, *this very moment* unpacking what has just arrived – the gold medals for the Darlings – when my man informs me they are actually in the castle! What a pleasure! How clever of you, my dear!'

The Duchess pointed to us, standing close together – I had without knowing I was doing it stationed myself near to Father.

'His Grace, Hugh, Duke of Northumberland,' she said. 'Mr and Miss Darling.'

I dropped a curtsy to the Duke, as best I could, and as I rose he took my hand, and said to me very feelingly, 'The honour is all mine, Miss Darling. All mine. Now you must come at once to my study, and see what I have for you. I have been at such pains that they should be just right . . . come, Charlotte.'

And he led us away again, down more corridors crammed with fine things. The Duke's library was the finest treasure I had yet seen. It was a tall room lined with books so high there were steps placed ready to reach them. My eye wandered over the shelves, but the Duke wished us to contemplate the leather boxes lying in a heap of crumpled tissue on the table. The Duke opened them with a flourish, and showed us two lovely golden discs like huge golden coins, lying in beds of satin within the dark boxes.

'The vellums are not here yet,' he told us. 'There are to be vellums, bearing citations, but they are not yet come. I give myself the pleasure of presenting the medals to you this minute – and I will send the vellums as soon as they are to hand.'

'Whom are we to thank for this great favour, sir?' Father said.

'The Royal Humane Society, of which I am vice president. The vellums are to say' – here he rustled in his papers and picked up a note – 'That the singular intrepidity, presence of mind and humanity which nobly urged GRACE HORSLEY DAR-LING to expose her life in a small boat to the impending danger of a heavy gale of wind and tremendous sea, etc. etc., and the extraordinary fortitude which she heroically displayed throughout the whole of that hazardous undertaking . . .'

I was blushing deeply.

'Come, Northumberland, you overwhelm her,' said the Duchess. 'Shall we have your medal sent back to be drilled for a ribbon that you may wear it?'

My heart shrank at the thought. I had no occasion for a silk mantle – when would I wear a gold medal? I will not deny my joy at it. But I wanted to have it in my trinket-box; not to wear it!

'It is so lovely a thing, ma'm,' I said. 'The design so beautiful, I think it would be a pity to drill it.'

'We could have it put in a glass locket, so you might wear it that way! Capital idea! I shall see to it myself,' said the Duke. 'Now, Grace, what do you think of it?'

'We have already had silver medals, sir,' I said. How difficult to answer him! 'I did not think we were to have gold ones also. Is it not, perhaps . . . is it not too much?'

'Too much?' he said. Then he took a step towards me, and said, 'My dear Miss Darling, of all my people you are the bravest. That you should act as you did when the occasion found you, in the midst of the gentle domestic cares of a female – that you were found ready, and did not hesitate – the gold medal is entirely right, and in no way too much, believe me.'

'A gold medal is very well, Northumberland,' said the Duchess. 'But should we not try to be of more practical help? The attention of the public is becoming burdensome, there is endless talk about the funds, and there is that unfortunate matter about the circus.'

At those words I felt myself begin to tremble. I would rather have died than have made some error of conduct that was known to the Duchess!

Father said, 'That has indeed distressed us. It was my daughter's intention merely to sit among the spectators, and enjoy the show. There was no call for anyone to accuse her of wishing to compete for attention with Mr Batty's quadrupeds!'

'From the sound of things Mr Batty is a good-hearted man, but of low degree. He perhaps did not understand the impropriety of the proposed visit,' said the Duke.

'Sir, I am beset every day by such requests,' I told him. 'I am very loath to offend or disappoint people, especially when they have been kind . . . but they are too many . . .'

'You must refer any request that troubles you to me,' said the Duke. 'You must regard me as your Guardian.'

I was terrified at the thought. 'Oh, sir!' I said. 'I do not in the least wish to be a trouble to anyone!'

'The Duke has many means at his command,' the Duchess said. 'He has secretaries to write letters. He has an invaluable and unrivalled grasp of affairs. And he has no daughter' – how strange that she should say 'he has no daughter', and not 'we have none'! – 'You may trust him, Miss Darling, as a father to you.'

'I am not in need of a father, ma'm,' I said to her, 'I have a much-loved and respected father of my own!' I did not say, you would have trouble getting me into a coble to row with Duke Hugh Percy! but I thought it.

'My dear young lady, of course you have!' said the Duke. 'And your sentiments do you the utmost credit. But have you not just this minute confessed yourself perplexed by the requests you are receiving?'

We made him no reply. My father did not speak up and say he could manage such matters for me. After a moment, the Duke said, 'Let us call for a dish of tea, and let us sit down together and talk this over between us, as though it were all within the family. How do you say?'

We agreed. The Duke had us sit down in great armchairs by a small fire burning in a huge hearth at one end of the library, and a servant brought tea in a silver pot, poured into cups so fine the light showed shadows of my fingers through the china. The Duchess drank her tea very rapidly, and then said, 'If you are talking business, Northumberland, I shall retire. Shall Miss Darling come with me?'

'I think not,' said the Duke. 'I think she should hear what is said. Find her a suitable book to look in, Charlotte, before you go, in case she is bored.'

The Duchess brought me a book of birds. The plates in the book were in rich colour, and most finely done. Each page showed cock and hen birds, and eggs, and in the sky at the top of the page an outline of the bird seen far off in flight. I had never seen such a book before in my life, and it filled me with joy. I turned the pages, and listened to the talk.

'You will hardly be used to the management of sums of money such as are in prospect for your daughter now,' said the Duke, putting down his cup, and with a wave of the hand causing the servant to remove the tea-things and depart.

'There's the money we have received,' said Father carefully, 'and the money being talked of. What we have received is not out of the way for me. I doubt of being confused by it. What is being talked of is another thing. And it does seem out of my power, Your Grace, although I have tried, indeed I have, to see justice done, or even talked of, between ourselves and the lifeboat men.'

'Exactly,' said the Duke. 'But it is within my power. I am well aware how jealous that class of persons is over scrupulous justice in money matters, especially when they trust to their superior's sense of honour. I would be very glad to discuss the sums with you, Darling. Will you favour me by confiding in me what money you have been paid directly?'

'To this date I have received thirty pounds, and my daughter one hundred pounds, including the gift from the Queen made to her today,' Father said. 'And the boatmen have been paid five pounds between them, by Mr Smeddle.'

The Duke rose, and taking down an account book, laid it upon the table and wrote these figures down.

'I have sent the boatmen two guineas a man myself, last se'enight,' he said, 'so I reckon they have had some three pounds each. I am as concerned as you are, Darling, about them. Brave fellows, of course. I have been at pains to make sure wherever possible that they are included in the head of the subscriptions. Now, my inquiries as to how much money, and held by whom, is collected, lead me to think we shall have at least three hundred pounds to distribute. I propose to divide the sum, when the fund is closed, into three equal parts; one for you, one for your daughter, and one for the boatmen. And I imagine that gifts will continue to arrive at the Longstone; the public enthusiasm shows no sign of abating. So . . .' he was scribbling on a sheet of paper, which he passed across the table to my father – 'that would produce, if we have guessed future amounts correctly, something like this.'

Father looked at the paper. 'This gives to my daughter thirty times what each man in the lifeboat will get,' he said.

'But a large part of the largesse for your daughter comes directly to her from the public. We cannot regard the lifeboat as having some claim on presents made to your daughter, or indeed to you.'

'But as regards the money in the funds, Your Grace. Might it not be divided equally between all nine of us who that day risked our lives?' Father said.

I was turning a page between a gloriously coloured parrot from Brazil, and a humming-bird in dazzling colours — my hand froze and the page remained unturned while I listened.

'I hardly think so, Darling. It is your daughter's deed which has touched the public heart and opened their purse strings. There will be a scandal if they think the money has not gone where they wished it to go. And the plain fact is the lifeboat did not rescue anybody, because nobody remained to be rescued! Besides, Darling, man to man I will confess to you that I am very concerned about this. The lifeboat men will already be grossly overpaid, and I am afraid this may produce resentment in future rescues from shipwreck.'

'I fear resentment now, sir,' Father said.

'Well, well. I will consult with Archdeacon Sharp about it, and make sure that the Crewe Trustees are in agreement,' said the Duke. 'But I think myself that an equal division of three parts will best serve. Which brings us back to the question of Grace's money. I will willingly act as her Guardian in this matter, and set up a trust to manage it for her. We can invest the bulk of it in the three-percents, and leave a sum available to her in case of need. She may have the interest paid to her regularly. She will need to make a will. I shall consult my lawyers, if you will allow me, and get these matters organized.'

'Thank you, sir,' said Father.

'Grace – have you understood what we were talking of?' said the Duke. 'Do you agree to it?'

'If Father thinks it best,' I said.

'Good, good,' said the Duke, 'that's settled then. Now, Darling, if my rank in life puts me in a position to know better than you can do how to deal with trusts, and suchlike, the boot is on the other foot about boats at sea. I would appreciate your advice to me about another matter. There can be no man who knows the Ferne Islands as you do, and the Fernes are the cause of the larger part of the shipwrecks on my coast; I am very disturbed that the lifeboat provided at Sunderland could not be launched when it was needed.'

'It is too large a boat, sir,' said Father.

'It has been suggested to me that an exchange might be effected between the lifeboat at Holy Island, and the one at Sunderland. I am told the bigger boat would launch more easily from Holy Island, and the smaller one might be got down the slope at Sunderland in the face of the severest weather.'

'That is right on both counts, sir,' Father said. 'But the mistrust of the lifeboat, and the preference of men for a coble such as they are daily familiar with, may not be quickly overcome.'

'But you do recommend the exchange of boats?'

'Yes; it can do no harm, and it will please the Sunderland men that their inability to use the boat provided has been attended to.'

'I thank you,' said the Duke.

As we were leaving he summoned Mr Blackburn to show us the castle and grounds, and taking leave of me, he took my hand, and said, 'You are to refer to me in every difficulty, Miss Darling. And be especially careful in the case of suitors; there will be fortune-hunters, there will certainly be fortune-hunters! Now I come to think of it, you should refer all such requests to me, like unwelcome requests to make visits. I shall be glad to arbitrate.'

And then at last we were with the wholly unalarming Mr Blackburn, and free to walk in the Duke's gardens. My grandfather Horsley was gardener to the Castle at Balmboro', and I love gardens, and was glad to see fruit and flowers, and ask questions.

Mr Blackburn said, 'You should not be in awe of the Duke, Miss Darling, beyond what his station demands. He is most kind. You will be well served with such a protector.'

'It is his kindness that most alarms me, Mr Blackburn,' I said, but he merely smiled, and led us back through the mighty buildings to the town gate.

There was a great press of people outside the gate. And the moment the servants opened the doors for us an uproar began. The crowd was crying and cheering and stretching out their hands, and jostling each other as they pressed towards us. I shrank back. They looked like nothing so much as the people stranded on Harker all desperate to clamber into the coble, who had scared me so. It took me a moment to realize that we ourselves were the cause of the hubbub.

Two of the Duke's people ran forward shouting, 'Make way there! Let people come out!' And we got a little way. Then those at the back trying to get a glimpse of us pushed forward again. Hands reached out to touch me on every side, fingers tugged at my dress and shawl, and there was an uproar of voices. From the back of the crowd a young man's voice called 'Bravo! Bravo the Darlings!' and this was taken up with deafening applause. A young woman was pressed so hard against the railings that she fainted, and in the diversion of attention this caused Father put an arm round my waist, and holding me firmly, thrust me through the crowd. We made no attempt to go forward, but he took me moving sideways, crabways. I think once we were among the people we disappeared from the general view, and they did not know which way to jostle. We wriggled and pushed through the people, until we were in the thick of the crowd.

Seeing us trying to escape the throng someone said to us, 'Did ye see them? Did ye catch a glim o' the bonnie anes? Are they yonder?' There were tears in her eyes. 'Aye,' said Father grimly, thrusting past her. And all this while I was terrified. I thought we should have been crushed to death, and the shouting seemed like the screams of gulls when they flock and fight over the carcasses of fish.

'Bear up, Gracie. Nearly there,' Father whispered to me, and suddenly we were free, we had come out behind the backs of the crowd. Somebody turned and saw us, and cried, 'There they are! There!' and as everyone turned we took hands and ran down Narrowgate, plunging into the little greengrocer's shop like children at Barley-breaks gaining the safety of base.

It was safety only of a kind. Our cousins MacFarlane who kept the shop had a dinner waiting for us, but also a gathering of friends, good people of the town, upon whom they depended for their trade, who had all been promised a few words with us. I was so shaken and crumpled that I would have given much for a few moments of quiet, but how could I other than seem pleased to be introduced to Miss Blackburn, whose father had so kindly escorted us through the castle just since, or any other friend of my cousins?

But the street outside the shop was now packed with people, all knocking on the door and window panes, and calling us by name. Mr Blackburn came in by the back gate to the shop, and went out to the crowd, asking them to go home, but nothing would satisfy until he agreed that I would show myself at the upstairs window, which I was loath to do, for it seemed like seeking attention. My cousin MacFarlane, however, asked me to do it, before his windows were pushed in and somebody was hurt, and so I went upstairs to the bedroom, and Father opened the window, and we leaned out and waved to the mob below.

I looked down at a sea of upturned faces, bright in the late afternoon light. When I was among them they had seemed to me in the grip of frenzy, mad as gulls; now I looked down at them I saw that they were sincere; a feeling rapture lit their gazing eyes, and their love was as sensible as sunlight. I felt their love as a great blessing of which I was unworthy, weighing upon my heart. They fell quiet on seeing us in the window, and then a lone voice began to sing a Chapel hymn, and others took it up till the street rang with it:

> *'While the nearer waters roll,*
> *While the tempest still is high:*
> *Hide me, O my Saviour, hide,*
> *Till the storm of life is past;*
> *Safe into the haven glide,*
> *O, receive my soul at last!'*

and little by little the greater part of the crowd went away singing:

> *'Plenteous grace with thee is found,*
> *Grace to cover all my sin,*
> *Other refuge have I none . . .'*

Yet a few were still lingering hours later. We delayed our going home, till the crowd should have dispersed, and Father was anxious that we should miss the Berwick coach which would set us down at Belford, a possible walk to Balmboro', by which we had intended to get home. He saw how I trembled at the thought of facing the street again before it was deserted. And yet we did get home that night, and easily too, for a little before five there was a knock at the MacFarlanes' door, where a conference was going on as to whether we should go or stay, and an ostler presented himself. He said his master was a gentleman of Alnwick, whose coach and pair stood at our disposal, to drive us to Sunderland or Balmboro' whenever we should wish to depart. If the attention I have been given has often been as welcome as a storm at sea, I have also known true useful kindness.

It was dark when we got to Balmboro', and there was a soft mist on the shore. So Mother and Brooks would have to wait till morning for the tale of our great day; we would lodge with Thomasin. Father walked up to the castle to see if he could see his light; he hated to be away from it. And I was left talking to my sister beside her little fire. I told her all the Duke had said, as closely as I could remember it, even to where he warned me against fortune-hunters:

'But, oh, Thomasin!' I said. 'I will marry without consulting *him*!'

'Will you now?' she said, laughing. 'And who is it to be, Gracie? Do I know him?'

I said nothing. 'Life is hard on a woman,' said Thomasin after a while. 'She who marries must be ruled.'

'Father rules us. We are used to that,' I said.

'And I bridled at it sometimes, as well you know.

But Father rules us with love, Gracie. You should hear the tales of woe my customers tell me, standing here being pinned, and measured! It would make you think twice, indeed it would. That mighty Duke of yours perhaps knows a thing or two . . .'

'Since when have you been respectful of your betters, Thomasin?' I said. 'I am going up now, for I am *woeful swere*, such a day it has been.'

'Off with you then. But if you are to be the next of us married, you'll have your work cut out catching up with Brooks, mind!'

'What do you mean, Thomasin? What do you know?'

'It'll keep, dear. Goodnight.'

Tired as I was I could not sleep. My feelings were buffeted like the coble in a storm, thinking over the day. I dwelt first on the Duke proposing that I consulted him over offers of marriage. I was at once in awe of him and indignant at him. Father had not spoken up and defended us. What *was* it Mr Reay had said about Father being nonplussed? On an impulse I took up a pen and a sheet of paper from the little writing-table in the corner of the bedroom, where Thomasin sat to write, and penned a letter to Mr Reay.

Dear Mr Reay, I wrote,
When we parted I promised to write to you if ever I changed my mind. My mind is now greatly changed, and I would gladly make you a different answer should you return for it, as you said you would.
    GHD, Balmboro'. December 20th.

When I had written this I lay down. I was still weary, but calmer in my mind. I lay thinking of the cities and the glories of the world, of every place far from Longstone; how perhaps there might be other ways to see zebras and elephants, besides going to Mr Batty's circus; and of a young man with flaxen hair. Oddly, I could not call his face to mind. I must have paid no better attention to his true appearance than he had to mine.

Then I thought of the golden medal that was mine, and of Father saying, 'My daughter will be paid thirty times what the boatmen get,' and the Duke saying, 'the whole are grossly overpaid.' Had he said that? And when at last I fell asleep I dreamed. I dreamed I was in my bed in the lighthouse. A great wind was blowing, and a huge sea running, I could hear it. I woke to hear Thomasin breathing quietly in the bed beside me; 'Why does she not wake?' I thought. Then I realized that the sound I heard was the wind in the great trees just below the cottage, and the light of the moon, playing peek-a-boo with the scudding clouds, and neither the waves nor the lighthouse beams. Again I drifted off to sleep. I seemed to be in the Longstone. I got up. A faint light as of dawn breaking shone upon me. I moved to the window, and saw the dark bulk of the great wreck looming up from the glassy sea. And there beside it on the rocks I saw nine golden sovereigns, gleaming. I ran down the stairs, crying, 'A wreck, Father! A wreck!' I was calling, and he, drawing on his trews as he answered, said, 'Now God help us, and Brooks away!'

He ran up the stairs towards me, holding his unfastened trousers with one hand, and buttoning his shirt with the other. So I regained the lantern with my father at my back, and together we looked out. Father stood beside me, and played his glass upon the scene.

'Can we get them, Father?' I said.

'If we're quick enough,' Father replied.

And then I woke, trembling. And once more it was long before I slept.

In the morning sense returned to me. I knew well enough that we had not thought of the premiums – there had been no time to think of anything but wind and tide – and yet the image lingered with me, and would not leave me, of the dark rock, and clinging to it not the poor desperate people we had really seen, but coins, golden coins, with their perilous bright sheen.

· 15 ·

We had soft weather towards Christmas. There were many days of delicate pale mist – a grey mist with a smidgeon of lilac to it – and gentle swell, as though the sea were thoughtful, half asleep. Instead of tearing itself into furies over the rocks of our islands, it drew their outlines dozens of times a day on each rising and each falling tide, brimming quietly in each ragged crevice, blashing quietly in and out of the low-tide pools. There was a great profusion of birds; ducks' flesh and feather the most we could eat or use, and some for Father to send as presents to friends on shore.

All day and every day the boats came over from Sunderland and from Balmboro', bringing visitors, until we longed for storms. At times our rooms seemed as crowded as the streets at Alnwick. And I was driven distracted by them. All saying the same things, asking the same things, the women and girls all wanting to touch me, and to have keepsakes. There was nowhere in the tower I could withdraw from them, but I was on view until the last of them departed. Some of them, coming from Sunderland, complained to us loudly that someone or other in Sunderland had made light of the rescue, had asserted it was nothing, that anyone could have done it. They seemed unshaken in their view of us as heroic, only angry that anyone could think otherwise. I never answered any such complaint, and Father took to answering it with an estimate of the wind force that morning on the Beaufort scale, remarking courteously that the lighthouse was not provided with a scientific anemometer (which the Trinity Brethren soon put right), so that he was trusting to his long experience for his guess at it.

Mr Tulloch gave me help. All this while he had lodged with us, keeping out of the way when he could, and spending time when the weather and tides allowed him, stationed on Harker Rock, until the very last remnants of the wreck were washed away, and nothing was there for him to watch over. Otherwise he sat long hours in the storeroom, from the window of which he could see the site of the calamity. He had salvaged a deal of timber, and some panels from the ship, which were found floating long after there was little left to see above the water, and though he had made report to Lloyd's – Father helped him with that – they took no note of the last remaining timber, but sent him a letter of discharge. Then he offered to repay our kindness to him by three days' carpenter's work before he should leave – he offered to board in the staircase to the lantern where it rose through the sitting-room and the bedchambers, so that it might be possible to have some seclusion, even with strangers going up and down.

We could not have made a change to the fabric of

the lighthouse without permission, but by good fortune the Trinity boat called on us the day after the offer was made. They came to see all was well, and they found us with our duties discharged, and everything clean, but with visitors thronging the rocks and all our rooms. Father asked if Mr Tulloch might enclose the stair, the need for it being clearly to be seen, while strangers trooped through the bedrooms. And when they learned how cheaply it might be done – at no expense at all to Trinity House – they gave permission at once, leaving Father a written docket of approval.

Mr Tulloch worked most ingeniously. There was no window for the stair through my room, but it had relied on the light of the open chamber. Mr Tulloch cut holes in the boarding to admit light to the stair, that it might be safe, but he cut the holes at the level of each second tread, that were too low to peep through. And then this is how we managed; when a boat was seen coming I withdrew to my room. Mother welcomed people – there could never be too many people for her, it seemed! Father showed them the lighthouse, and took them aloft, the door to my room being closed, and showed them the lantern, the machinery, the view from the balcony; pointed out the spot of the wreck, and the route we had taken to reach it. While everyone was aloft I would slip down to the sitting-room and then as they came down they would find me sitting quietly at my sewing, and could linger a few moments and speak to me. I would smile if I could, answer if I could, and then Father would show them to their boats again.

Mr Tulloch brushed away thanks when he left us, but he was distressed. 'I ought to be glad to be away from the scene of death,' he said. 'But I am not. I am gripped like a rabbit that stares at a snake. And your kindness . . .' He seemed too distressed to go on.

'Fresh scenes will cheer you,' Father said.

'I cannot forget . . .'

'There, there, man. Swann is waiting to take you.'

And he was gone.

There was no relief from the visitors, except in times of storm. And there was no relief from the flow of letters and presents. I have loved presents, both giving and getting of them since I was a child, and it gives me joy to find or make some little thing as a gift. But the most of these presents were not useful. And everyone needed an answer, every letter, however silly, demanded an hour of me to make reply. I soon found that leaving them lying would not do; as it was the weather made many things late in reaching or late in leaving us; if in addition something waited long for my attention soon there was a second and a third letter from the correspondent, and I had need to make many excuses for the delay.

Whoever wrote Father's copy book had thought of a need for a letter in thanks for a Bible – I had now enough Bibles to furnish a whole diocese of churches – but had not thought of most of what I struggled with.

What could I say to sheafs of poems? Though some were by very famous men – there was even one by the great poet Mr Wordsworth – they did not seem very sensible to us. One, for an example, sent to us out of the *Berwick & Kelso Warder*, read:

> On Miss Grace Horsley Darling.
> Tho' hoarsely she has heard the flood
> Contending with the wind,
> With naught to cheer her solitude,
> Nor to her race to bind
> Yet she by nature seems endowed
> Though on a rock enshrined
> To be the Grace of womanhood,
> And Darling of mankind!

We puzzled over it, till Father remembered that there were puns in Shakespeare, so he supposed they might not always be meant in jest. But 'on a rock enshrined'? *Enshrined?*

'Whoever wrote that had never visited a lighthouse, Gracie,' said Brooks.

'Never mind, Brooks,' said I. 'Soon there will be no person left in the entire kingdom who has not visited this one!'

And then what was I to say to gifts of novels? Father would never have them in the house. We spent an anxious half-hour considering if I might keep a copy of *Marmion*. At last Father said he supposed that Sir Walter Scott was so admired among the gentry, that there might be no harm in it. I put it on the lengthening row upon my shelf – I should have asked Mr Tulloch to make me a mile of shelves – beside the Methodist Hymnal, which we found has some good Sunday singing in it. I have not had time to read *Marmion*.

At least *Marmion* seems to be about the past, and any liberties it takes are with those long dead. 'Grace Darling, or the Maid of the Isles' by Mr Vernon, sent to me in parts, with a letter from the author, was supposed to be about me. 'From the miscellaneous nature of your reading you will often have discovered the reins given to fancy,' Mr Vernon told me. But as Father had interdicted novels, I had discovered no such thing. What an eventful childhood Mr Vernon's story made for me, and what a number of friends among the nobility! Friends? Lovers, rather. But Father has many booklets about shipwrecks, and I knew how they ought to be told.

Kind sir,
I received the ten numbers of The Maid of the Isles, *which you sent, and beg to return my sincere acknowledgements of the same; and being sensible of your good intentions I wish you every success in the world.*
PS. Although I have no wish for anything of the kind, permit me to say that a little book wrote after the manner of The Kent Indiaman, *or* The Rothesay Castle *would have been preferred by your much obliged humble servant,*

G. H. Darling.

That was that, then. I do not know what became of the ten parts, for I had them not to hand when many months later a gentleman wrote to me to know if this or that part of Mr Vernon's romancing was true. I thought it came so close to lying as made no difference.

What then could I say to a lady who wrote to me, 'we often fancy you in your little boat, enjoying the fury of the waves.' That stung me to answer:

You requested me to let you know whether I felt pleasure to be out in a rough sea which I can assure you there is none, I think, to any person in their sober senses. I have seven apartments in the house to keep in a state fit to be inspected every day by gentlemen, so that my hands are kept very busy, and I never think the time too long, but often too short. I have often had occasion to be in the boat with my father for want of better help, but never at the saving of life before, and I pray God, may never be again . . .

And least welcome to me of all, there was also a new kind of letter, from the Duke or his lawyers, about money, and trusts, and wills.

I should have learned to hate letters had it not been for those we had from friends. We heard from Mr Watson. He said to tell Brooks that he was busy painting the barracks, but had not yet been driven mad. He had devised what he called a 'Panorama', pictures to be shown in the theatre, and was touring it around and wondered if we might visit Hull, and see it. But he had to make do with Mr Donovan, who was with him, and prospering mightily as a famous survivor.

We heard from Mr Parker that he had a daughter and had called her little Grace, as he had promised. His wife was glad and proud to name her so, he said. But there was no letter from John Reay.

The dream of the guineas gleaming on the rock revisited me, several times.

At Christmas people stay at home. The roads are sticky, the nights early, and everyone has family to think of. We had a little rest from being visited. By strangers, that is, for at Christmas my brothers and sisters come home all who can, like birds of winter, and we look forward to it all year.

The Christmas of 1838 we saw everyone; my sister Betsy, who is in service in Sunderland, got leave of absence for three days, and my married sister Mary-Ann came with her babe, Georgian, and all the brothers arrived, William, the eldest, who is a joiner in Alnwick, and Robert, who is a mason at Belford, with their wives, and George from the ship-yard at Newcastle, and Thomasin, of course, and we were all very merry together. There were willing hands to share the tasks, and the baby to rock and lullaby, and it was mild fair weather for the season, so we could get out and scramble on the rocks, and the men could shoot wildfowl.

At night we crowded round the fire, and there was much talk of shipwreck and of rescue, and most of it was not about the *Forfarshire*, but of the Christmas four years since, which was with wild weather, when a sloop called *Autumn* out of Peterhead was lost. That time Father with William and Robert and George rowed out to the Knavestone, and got a man off the rock. A man called Logan. That was done at great hazard; my brother Robert jumped overboard, and swam with a rope's end between his teeth, which he fastened to Logan, and remained behind standing where Logan had stood. It took a long time to get the rope thrown to Robert. Logan having stood nearly ten hours was half dead and frozen, and could do nothing, and the tide was making. In the struggle to get the rope to Robert without holing the boat both oars were lost, but at last a trick of the wind's relenting had the rope in Robert's hands, and he was pulled back into the boat, badly scraped, but whole. Then they thought, being without oars they must sail, and could only go before the wind to Holy Island, but the wind changed about, and they got home, having laboured three hours. That time my only part was to have seen poor Logan standing to his knees in the swirling waters, upon the Knavestone Rock, and woken all the men.

'We never got into the papers for doing that,' Robert said.

'Why, nobody told the papers!' said Mary-Ann. 'They only print what they're told of.'

'I shall try telling them, when I get back to Newcastle,' said George. 'That would be a story really worth printing!'

'Oh, it'll be old news, Georgie. Too old,' said Mary-Ann wisely. But she was wrong, as it happened. George did get the Knavestone rescue printed in the papers, to my brothers' great satisfaction.

My brother William said to me, 'You're a good girl, Gracie. You take after your eldest brother, I hear!'

'Aw, it wasn't much, in spite of the fuss there is making,' said George.

'How do you know it wasn't much?' asked Thomasin.

'Because Gracie contrived it!' said George, ducking Thomasin's threatened blow.

One Christmas, oh, I am glad to say it, is much like another with us. We always shed a tear for my brother Job, dead these eight years since, who was swept away by consumption, and lies in Balmboro' churchyard. We always tell tales of the ghost of great St Cuthbert, which walks these beloved isles; we always have a kissing-bush of holly and ribbons and oranges, we always play hunt the thimble, and spice the hasty cakes, and give each other little gifts. Father reads the Christmas story in his Bible, and we row over to the Boxing Day service if the weather will let us.

That Boxing Day was calm enough, with a gentle swell, and a bright glisk on the waters. I sat between Thomasin and Mother, and my brothers rowed us briskly the length of the Fernes, and over the Inner Sound, and beached us below the castle. The bells were ringing, and we joined the people flocking to the church. The Balmboro' folk were glad to see us. They smiled. They greeted me, more especially than they used, but they have known me all my life, and there is no frenzy about it, no goose-flesh. Mr Smeddle bustled up to us in his best frock-coat, and introduced us all to the new parson as though we had been the first family of the parish, but I am used to Mr Smeddle now – it was George who blushed!

After the service, we rowed back, and William Swann was coming out at the same time from Sunderland, so that we all arrived together. 'We did not look to see you over the holiday, Mr Swann,'

Mother said. 'What, are you after a better slice of figgy pudding than your own wife makes?'

'I've got such a grand box here as I didn't like to keep waiting,' William Swann said. 'I'm off again to my own figgy pudding right away, now, but I'll take a slice of yours in hand, Goody Darling, since you offer!'

We all stood round staring at the grand box – a crate, no less, and from the Duke. When the lid was off the first thing on top of the straw was a letter to Father:

'List of things sent in the box to William Darling,' Father read. As he read Betsy and Mary-Ann, eager as children, went down on their knees one each side of the box and began to pull off the straw and unpack the parcels.

> *'Medal from the Shipwreck Society at Newcastle.*
> *A coat – jacket – trousers and cloth for D. "That's me, I think," of waterproof cloth.*
> *2 votes of thanks on vellum (framed) from the Humane Society.*
> *For Mrs Darling.*
> *A silver teapot to be constantly used by her, and afterwards to belong to Grace H. Darling.*
> *Camlet cloak, waterproof. 4 pounds of tea.'*

'Oh, William! A silver teapot!' Mother said, as Betsy put it into her hands. 'It's nicer than what my mistress has,' Betsy said, admiring. 'And more tea than we afford in a six-month!'

'Whist, woman, there's more,' Father said, turning the paper over.

'*For Grace Horsley Darling.*
A silver-gilt watch with a gold seal and two keys.
A medal from the Shipwreck Society at Newcastle.
Camlet cloak, waterproof.
*A prayer book with daily lessons from both
testaments.*
Volume with the best notes to accompany the Bible.
One of the vellum notes of the Humane Society.'
With that the box was empty but the note was
not finished.
'*NB. The two medals, the watch seal, and keys are
in the inside of Mrs Darling's teapot. The prayer
book sent by her Guardian may be very convenient
to those who are detained at the lighthouse on Sundays.*

*The notes on the Bible are the best that have been
published.*

N.'

'But where's the watch?' asked George. 'I want to
see the watch!'

'*I* want to put on Father's waterproof!' said
Robert.

What a hubbub! The watch was found in a nest
of straw, too hastily pulled out, wrapped in soft
leather, and very handsome, large and plain. Another
note was with it.

'Come, Gracie, what's in yours? Read us yours!'
cried Mary Ann.

I read: '*The watch if constantly worn by my Ward,
Grace Darling, will go remarkably well.*

'*To wind up* . . . – It's telling me how to wind it
up.'

'Read it, read it! How are you to wind it up?'
This from William, no longer standing aloof.

'*Take hold of the ring with the finger and thumb,*' I
read, '*holding the face of the watch downwards, and press
the thumb-nail against the spring at the end of the pillar.
The back will then fly open –*'

'It does indeed,' said Father, who had picked up
the watch, and was following the actions as I read.

'*with the key wind from right to left, that is, looking
south; wind from west to east . . .*'

But instead of winding Father began to laugh,
and I to laugh with him, until we were all near
helpless with mirth.

'Mind you make a note, Gracie,' said Father, at
last, wiping his eyes with his knuckles, 'when you
look south, west is on your right, and east is on your
left! Remember it at all times, girl, not just when
you're winding a watch – it'll come in handy, knowing that, living on a lighthouse!'

'He hasn't written you are to let go the knob
when you're done winding it!' said Mary-Ann.

'Oh, you be fine and careful with that watch,
Grace!' Robert said. 'Don't you go thinking that
just because you can see to a revolving light you can
wind a watch easy!'

'I dare say the Duke didn't think of that, in his
great castle,' said Mother complacently. She had
done with gloating over the teapot, and was con-
tentedly looking at the caddy full of tea, which was
in a painted box, with pictures of whales. 'There's
no call to mock,' she added – a hopeless appeal.

'Make us tea, Mother! Let's see how it tastes out

of silver!' Father said. And while it was mashing, the men folk all ran into the cold and open, and putting on Father's waterproof gear each in turn they slopped buckets of seawater over each other, and emerged triumphantly dry.

'Heavier than oiled linens, but vastly tighter against water,' said William, coming in at last for his tea. 'I envy you those drop-dries a deal more than Gracie's notes on the Bible. But did you read the Duke called himself your Guardian, Grace? What's that, then?'

'He offered; there's no naysaying a Duke, William,' Father said. 'And with the whole world rhyming on about her, it may do good.'

'You didn't know I'm a Duke's ward, William? You'll have to mind your manners with me now,' said I.

My sisters and I were all sleeping hugger-mugger in my room together, and so I had put all the money I had been given – the crisp bank notes, the shining guildies, into my thrift-box, out of sight. But even so I dreamed again of waking, and looking out. At first I saw just what I remembered – the awful sight of the great bulk of the ship, the faint discernible movement of living souls moving on the dark rocks under the curtains of spray thrown by the great waves. But as I watched, the dim shapes of men were transformed into golden discs, shining like the rising sun, and I heard myself say to Father, 'Can we get them?' and he said, 'If we are quick! Be quick!' Then I woke, with my contentment as broken as my sleep.

And I thought, 'It is the money in my box that troubles me. I never had money before; I will have none now; I will give every farthing away, and sleep sweetly as I used to before!' This thought was balm to me, and I fell asleep without dreaming more till Father woke me for the dawn watch. Then moving stealthily so as not to wake a soul, I took the thrift-box with me, and went aloft. I checked the lamps, I timed the turning machinery that swept the beam round, holding my new watch in my hand. All was well. Father always left all well before he woke me, as though our lives depended on it, and as though our lives depended on it, I always checked things at once, lenses, rotation, wicks, oil.

I waited for the intermittent light of the lantern to be overtaken by the steady light of day. And it dawned a colour of deepest chrome yellow, like molten gold, in which the sovereigns I tipped out upon the floor of the walkway showed no brighter than brass pennies, for everything alike looked guinea-gold, and the banknotes as though on gold leaf. I divided the money out, equally as near as it would go, with the small bawbees for baby Georgian. I took out curl-papers, and wrapped the money up, writing a name on each twist of paper – William and Ellen, Robert and Janet, Mary-Ann, Betsy, Thomasin, Brooks, George, baby. Then I ran downstairs, and tumbled the papers among the breakfast plates, set ready for the morning meal.

And then I climbed again, and watched the day lighten over the sea, the land swim gently into view in a shadowy haze, the white birds gliding, the rising sun striking suddenly the tower on the Brownsman, and then the light on Inner Ferne, and the ruins of the chapel and tower, and last the far-off bulk of Balmboro' Castle, with the little church to the right of it.

I watched with a lightening heart as the rich gold of the dawn thinned and paled to citron, and then to primrose, and then to the colourless brilliance of day, until all round me the vistas were of blue and white, and the lilac and umber shades of land; of every colour but gold.

· 16 ·

The money caused a commotion at breakfast. My sisters accepted theirs easily, and George took his joyfully, and kissed me for it. But William and Robert were minded to refuse the gift, and return it to me, and while we were disputing Father came in with Brooks, and found the argument ongoing.

'What do you say, Father?' asked Robert. 'Should we be taking, or Grace be giving money?'

I saw Father's brow darken at the question, and I spoke quickly. 'My brothers are glad enough to take shirts and warmers from me when I have had time to sew and knit. And do not we Darlings always share what we have?'

'The money is hers,' Father said to William. 'And hers to keep is hers to give. She may do what she likes.' But I thought he would rather I had not done it, nevertheless.

Then Brooks took up his paper from the table and put it unopened in his pocket. 'That's not *all* for the landlord of the Ship, mind,' I said to him.

'I'm wiser than I was, Gracie,' he said. 'Haven't you noticed?'

After Christmas the family dispersed, and we were left to the storms of the winter, and the household quietness those storms gave us. And that other storm – the storm of notoriety that beat about my head, and gave me no peace – was also in a lull. I hoped it had blown over; but it was to resume again with renewed force in the spring.

For a while, though, we had peace; saving for the stream of letters from the Duke and his lawyers. Everything had to be explained to me, set before me for my agreement, and to everything they suggested I consented. There was to be a trust; all the money given for me was to be invested, and I could draw upon the interest. Father explained to me how if I did not draw interest it would remain in the funds, and they would grow into good round sums. That seemed a good plan to me. I heartily wished for fewer letters about money; each time I had one to answer I dreamed again the terrible picture of the money lying on Harker, under the beating waves.

As to more invitations to me to go on shore, they came thick and fast as one wave after another. The Trinity wanted me to go to them for a presentation; the Mayor of Newcastle wanted me to go to receive money and thanks of the city; some distant cousins had been promising to show me to all their friends; but we had got canny, and Father said no for me. He was afraid that the Mayor of Newcastle might take offence, and he wrote very careful, saying I did not like to go about and show myself. But all was well, for the Mayor answered us kindly, and praised our common sense.

And then the spring came in, and with the spring the people came in droves. Three and four boats, sometimes five and six boats a day came out to us, so that the lighthouse was thronged with strangers till we could barely move a limb; we were as crowded as in the three days after the rescue, or more. It got worse as the weather got better, in a spring of flat calms and fair days, and it was all hen-flesh, all people staring and fingering, and making foolish remarks, so that it seemed to me that if I would not go to the circus, the world would make a circus of my home, where I would compete not with quadrupeds, but with the birds and seals.

There came no letter from John Reay.

Each morning I rose up in the dawn quiet, hope-ful, planning to get some little task done, some letter written to Thomasin or Betsy, or a friend; and then the day was harried and thronged, and nothing but the most needful work accomplished, so that I was hot and weary by the afternoon, and at night I slept fitfully, and was sweating when Father woke me. Brooks was again often on the mainland, and none could blame him.

At last I made excuse one morning to go to take a few little things to Betsy in Sunderland, or so I told Father. He let me go back with William Swann who had come out with provisions, on my saying I would come again with Brooks before nightfall. Mr Swann offered to land me on Balmboro' hard, and I had to insist to go to Sunderland, for he was loath to take me.

'Diven't yow linger on the quays, Miss Darling,' he said, as he brought us into the steps. 'I've summat to see to, and I cannot stay.'

I thought I would be hardened to be in crowds of people. And in Sunderland, where I have been coming and going all my life. I steeled myself to be surrounded with hubbub. But I was met with silence. As I walked towards the square aback of the quay, the bustle of the quays froze, the conversation died, eyes followed me. I stopped outside the Ship, and looked around, and raised my voice. I said,

'I am come to ask you, all the boatmen and fishermen, to bring not so many trippers out to Longstone. Not to come every day.'

There was a strange sound. They were hissing at me. The women who clean and pack the fish came thronging round me, hissing. The menfolk came behind them. Someone cried out from the gathering crowd:

'It's the cormorant girl!' Another voice said – I could not see the speaker – 'Aa' that money! Aa' that money for yow, and for our men little enough, next to nothing! Yow greedy wifey! And now yow come grudging the shillings they earn taking trip-pers, does yow? Yow'd stint them the earning a dozen shillings, and then?' And all the while the most of them hissing me, and their eyes blazing!

I ran away. I stumbled back up the slope, and they came after me, cat-calling, and throwing fish-heads. I was terrified. Then as I ran suddenly some-body pulled me hard by the sleeve, and I stumbled sideways, and found myself in the arms of a young woman, in a dark and narrow alleyway, who dragged me with her a few steps and thrust me into a doorway. The pelting sound of footfalls and yelling went past the end of the alley, and distanced as she shut the door. We were in a dark little room, with a tiny fire. I was weeping.

She put her arms round me, and said, 'There, hinny, there, be not frit.'

I wept on her shoulder, leaning on her plain brown dress, shaking. Someone racketed down the alley, shouting.

'Sit down, and I'll fetch us some ale,' she said. 'They'll soon give over.'

'This about the money is none of my doing,' I told her. 'I have never harmed anyone's purse, my life long; I know better what hardship is, indeed I do!'

'Of course yow haven't, hinny,' she said, bringing me ale in a grey pewter jar. 'I must think now how to get yow home. Best ask none of the boatmen.'

Just then came a knocking on her door, and a voice saying, 'Did you see what became of her? I have lost her!'

I shrank back in my chair, but the woman said, 'Oh, it's Thomas,' and drew the bolt. Thomas Cuthbertson came in, and closed behind him, wearing his seaboots and gear. He must have been on the quay, making ready to put out.

'Thank God!' he said, when he saw me. 'Are yow hurt, Miss Darling?'

I shook my head. I had taken no hurt that I could show him. 'They wouldna have more than pelted yow,' he said, 'but that's bad enough. We'd best get you home through Balmboro'. I'll borrow the landlord's horse at the Ship, and ride you there. I'll find Saburn to row you over. Will you come with me?'

I was recovering with the quiet and dark of the cramped little room, and the sips of ale. I nodded.

He came back shortly. He had tied the horse at the top of the alley. At the door I turned round to my rescuer, and said to her, 'Thank you for your kindness. To whom do I owe my protection?'

She said, 'I am Jane,' and then there passed between us a single glance of mystification, as I waited for her second name, and she saw that just 'Jane' left me waiting. Thomas said, 'Come now,' and we went to the horse's side, and he took me by the waist, and set me upon it, and mounted up behind me, and took the reins with his right hand, and held me fast with his left.

'Hold tight, Gracie; we're not going to linger!' he said, and kicked with heels at the horse's flanks. I was very shaken while we galloped; a coble sooner than a horse for me! But as soon as we were out of the town he reined in, and we went slowly along the road. The golden dunes were on our right, and beyond them the Fernes standing fair in the sunshine, and the Longstone far far out, white in the noonday light. The great bulk of the castle rose ahead of us, casting a shadow on the road as it turned round the foot of the castle mound, into Balmboro'.

'Will you go to your sister, Gracie, or to my mother to bide while I find a boat?' Thomas asked me.

'To your mother would be best,' I said. For Mrs Cuthbertson lived on the road into Balmboro', and I did not want to ride sitting up in front of Thomas the length of the town. She had a little tumbledown cottage, but sound and dry. She made me welcome to the best chair. Thomas told her what had happened, and she tutted, and shook her head, and said, 'They say money is poison, poison! They say it's the root of evil, Miss Grace; and I ken nowt about that for I've never had a penny to spare, all my life!' She smiled at me, pleasantly. And then, the moment the door closed upon Thomas, as he went to find Saburn, to carry me home again, she said, 'All that money, Miss Grace. It is ill-luck for Thomas; and I think fine it is ill-luck for yoursel.'

'It's a load on the spirit, I find,' I said to her.

'Do yow like my fairing?' she asked me, pointing at an object on her mantelshelf. 'My other son brought it from Newcastle. Take a look at it.'

It was an object in painted china, and it took me a moment to see that it was of me. A china lighthouse rose above curly china waves, and a little boat, more like a sauce-boat than a coble, placed among them, contained a figure of a girl with hair blowing out on the wind. I put it back hastily, and said, 'I was wearing curl-papers, Mrs Cuthbertson!'

'I thought yow mightna like it well,' she said. 'Thomas doesna like it. He would have asked for you by and by, Miss Darling, yow ken, but for the money. He will not ask now. He'll not be offering a fisherman's cottage to a woman of fortune.'

And before I could answer Thomas was there again, and he walked me a few yards towards the beach. I did not tell Saburn where I had been. I supposed everyone would get to hear of it, soon enough. And so they did; but since I had not spoken a word about it, Thomasin told me it as malicious gossip. Only Brooks looked at me strangely, and offered to go with me if ever again I had errands in Sunderland.

You may imagine my thoughts were troubled that night. I paced the walkway round the lantern, lingering aloft when the duties were done, watching the light pick out the endless heaving of the waves. It is not pleasant to be hated, and the unfairness of it stung me keenly. There was a smarting as before tears in my eyes when I thought of it, and a queer sort of catching in my chest.

Was it my fault if people made too much of me? My doing that they gave me money? Then a thought of dazzling simplicity came to me. No, it was none of my doing, and should remain none of my doing! The presents people gave me I should keep; but as for any money, I promised myself that I would never spend a penny of it. Had I rescued men only for greed? This was my perfect answer, my complete defence; the money should remain untouched. There should never be the smallest colour of justice to those cruel words thrown at me in Sunderland.

Then I thought further and knew I must use some cunning. The Duke was expecting me to ask for anything I needed, and I could not tell him I would live and die without needing a halfpenny piece; he would think it ungrateful, he might even think it a pride beyond my station. But it would be easy to outwit the Duke. I would write him a letter saying that I needed nothing at the present time, but that I might perhaps need something in June, or thenabouts . . .

and in June I would write the same again. He would think only that it was thrift, and be pleased with me!

What about Father then? Father would not think it sensible to foreswear the money, any more than he would have thought it sensible to spend it in a kenspeckled way that all the world might see. He had been keeping note of what it all amounted to, notes of who had given what, and which great Lord had contributed, with considerable satisfaction. This in order to be sure we did not fail to acknowledge favours, did not turn away an artist who was friend to a benefactor, for example, but he certainly expected me to benefit from the money, and I had best not tell him my mind, either. I wondered if he would still give me the purse he had always given me at quarter-days, in acknowledgement of the help he had of me in the lighthouse, and so that I might not need to ask for hairpins, as he put it. I thought perhaps he would no longer, and I was sorry then that I had given away every penny at Christmas. I must be careful not to lose my hairpins! I smiled, smiled at the breaking dawn. If need be I would do without hairpins, but I was resolved.

I thought, 'I will have a clear conscience, perfect certitude. It will be a fortress of calm for me, and I shall be happy again!' And so I was, for a day or two, until George's letter came.

He had written to Father and Mother, telling them the price of meat and flour in Newcastle, and how all the carpenters in the town were walking round on Whit Monday to make complaint, and he among them. He sent his clothes home to be mended, and he asked Mother to buy him more shirts and two suits of clothes. Everything in Newcastle, he wrote, was just to look and not to buy.

Mother and I had washed and ironed and mended and patched his shirts, and sent them away again with kind words, and telling him to send his things to me for washing and mending any time at need, and enclosing a little sugar and tea. And now he wrote again:

Dear sister,

I got your letter, and I was disappointed at Father not writing too, and I thought to myself I knew the reason of it, so therefore I could not help it. I was sorry to hear you could not do something for me, only that I send you the things. But dear sister, it is not so much that I need the things (therefore you know the reason of my not sending them). It is only about 30s. altogether that I owe but it is too much for me to make up . . . else, sister, you know I would never have asked you to do such a thing. It is to two or three persons that I am in debt, and the way that things are now I get nothing from the master at all, for they pay for my lodging and washing, and I have nothing through my fingers at all.

Dear sister, write immediately, and if you can do anything, send it with the carrier.
Your affectionate brother, George.

And now I was distraught and dreaming again. I rowed all around the shipwreck, finding thirty shillings on the rocks, and dropped it all into the deep as I strove to row back again, so I had nothing in my fingers at all. Those few days when I knew I would never touch the money, I had borne the admiration of the crowds of trippers very well, thinking, 'Well, they make too much of me, but I did do what it is they think I did, and to my own danger, truly.' So I smiled at them, and answered their questions calmly. But now I thought, 'Little they know that I am a greedy cormorant girl, that saw a chance to get money in the sufferings of others! Why don't they ask about me in Sunderland? Folk there would soon tell them what I am!' And I flinched and cringed inwardly under their words of praise, their greedy staring at me.

'You are looking peaky, Gracie,' Father said to me one morning at breakfasting. 'Is ought amiss that flesh and blood can help with?'

So partly against my better judgement, I brought out George's letter and showed him. While he read it over, frowning, I said, 'Father, I have hundreds of pounds if I ask the Duke for it, but I have not got thirty shillings!'

'Ask the Duke to pay George's debts?' cried Father, beating his fist upon the table. 'I forbid you, Grace!'

'But Father, I cannot bear he should be in trouble.'

'He will be in worse trouble if you send him money now, Grace. Once a sponge, always a sponge. He cannot live upon his sister, though his sister had all the tea in China. What – live upon his sister, and be a man?'

'But how will he do, Father?'

'Let him find for himself that it is easier to get into debt than out of it, Grace. That will be best for him. He is well set up with his master, if only he's careful, and he'll have his own money by and by. Mind now; don't go against me in this.'

'Go against you, Father? I said. 'When have I ever?'

'Ah, well, you're beyond my mastery now, Grace. Money and a guardian of your own − a will of your own you've always had. But George is in my charge. My son. Nothing to do with the Duke of any-where!'

Father sent me off then, to spend the day with Thomasin, and see if the land air would fetch a little colour into my cheeks. Thomasin and I talked over George's debt; we could not see how he could pay a debt of money out of found dinners and lodging, however he contrived.

'If Father forbids sending money, send something else,' said Thomasin.

'What could I send?'

'Something that's yours and no argument. Did you put a shawl on, when you went out to the *Forfarshire*?'

'My old brown one, full of holes.'

'Cut it up and send him the pieces.'

'But what . . . ?'

'He writes me that every shop-window in Newcastle is full of pictures of you, prints, fairings, ornaments, decorated boxes, figurines . . .'

'Ugh!' I said, shuddering.

'No doubt a scrap you were wearing on the

morning, with George to warrant for it, will bring something.'

Thomasin has a sharp wit to match her tongue. I sent George my shawl cut up, and I told him I would never ask him about it, but that if he took a farthing more than thirty shillings for the scraps, I would hold him no brother of mine, before the throne of judgement.

And by the next morning I had something other to think about, for Brooks came, bringing somebody with him; I saw from my window there was somebody in the coble with him, and I came down.

He brought 'Jane' into the kitchen with him, Jane my rescuer from the mob in Sunderland, and led her to Mother, and said, 'This is her, Mother.' And Mother jumped up and kissed her, and said, 'Welcome, daughter.'

Jane is older than Brooks; she can give him ten years, I would say. She is stocky, and her hands are worn with work, and her clothing respectable but shabby. She said she was better with a scrubbing-brush than a needle, and not afraid of work. But she said she was afraid of the sea; her father had drowned in a fishing-smack. She did not stay long that first time, and when Brooks came again, I asked him what he meant by it, getting himself ready to be a bridegroom, and telling me nothing about it.

'Yow've enough on your mind, Gracie,' he said. 'Yow hardly seem to be with us these days, what with writing grand letters, and fretting yowsel.'

'But I would like to have known, Brooks!'

'And what would you have said about her? She's

not very grand to be sister to a Duke's darling. And I know she is older. And I know she is plain, and hasn't twopence. I wouldna have yow have the chance to tell me aa' that in good time; and now it's too late, don't tell me.'

'But, Brooks, she is kind,' I said. 'She has lovely eyes. And Thomasin shall make her some better clothes.'

His face lit up. 'You think well of it, Gracie? I'm unco' glad!'

'Yes, I do, Brooks, apart from being surprised. But it's not to please me that you'll marry!'

'Well, now, dear sister,' he said, putting an arm round my shoulder, a thing not usual with him, 'I have had my eye on Jane for some time. I had thought I would wait a while, till the Trinity gave me official assistant keeper. But in asking her now you may credit it, I was thinking partly of you. Seems to me that another pair of hands would be welcome, and the sooner the better.'

'Don't I manage things well enough, Brooks?'

'You manage things gey fine, Gracie; but you often look weary. You'll have more time for your letters and a' that when I bring Jane.'

'But, Brooks, will you be happy?'

'She understands me,' he said. 'She'll look after me.'

· 17 ·

Brooks's wedding was the first of great changes in our family this two years past. Every one of them made us more thronged at home. We used to be so quiet here that any visitor made an interest for us; now we were so in the thick of our own lives we could have done well without even one stranger, leave alone several dozen a day! When the Trinity Brethren heard Brooks was married, they made him officially assistant keeper, and undertook to put up a house for him. While that was going forward they promised to wall round the foot of the tower, giving us a little sheltered yard that might keep the seas out of the kitchen. We looked forward to that.

Then there was talk of a new lighthouse on Coquet Island, some twenty-five miles south of us, where there had been many calamities. The Duke gave land to the Trinity to make a new light, and for all that Father might have said his sons were nothing to do with Dukes of anywhere, he was pleased enough when the Duke put forward my brother William's name to be the new keeper. The Duke told us in a letter that he was recommending William, for having been assistant to Father till he was sixteen, and being an honest, sober, quiet and industrious person, saying also that it was the Trinity that decided, but of course they took his word, and William had the job.

Bad luck as well as good befalls families. My sister Mary-Ann was widowed, and came home to us, bringing her babe Georgian, still in a cradle. My sister Betsy had left service, and came home to live till her husband-to-be could find a roof for her, and shortly after William sent his son, my nephew Billy, to be brought up alongside Georgian, till the bairn should have sense enough to be safe on Coquet Island, where there were cliffs and falls all round. William's wife was carrying another child, and sickly.

Now we were busy and noisy and crowded all day long, and the little laughter and little tears of babes flowed all round me like the seas. And I had no longer a room to myself, but must share with Betsy. My dreaming came and went, like the catching in my chest, and Betsy made complaint of me as a restless sleeper. I cannot disturb her as much as she does me, with her endless poking about among my things, trying to glimpse at my letters, asking questions. I am afraid of her catching me sending things to George; twice I have had to ask Thomasin to send to him with a few shillings from selling little things I have knitted, with apologies for getting no word from me, because Betsy has come bouncing in while I was writing, and asked what G. it was I wrote to, and I have been much put about. I must write my private letters in the dawn watch, now, crouched uncomfortably on the walkway round the lantern, and often growing cold, though I put on my shawl. But there is none to spy on me then, and all is quiet till little Georgian sets up her chat, and wakes the household.

When Brooks got married the Duke wrote to me:

Grace Darling,
As I am writing a letter to your father I must
inquire how my Ward is going on, and whether she
is in good health. I see by the papers that your
brother who jumped first into the boat at North
Sunderland, which went off to the wreck of the
Forfarshire, *is just married, are you going to follow*
his example?

I hope that the watch continues to go well, if it
should want cleaning you may let me have it when I
go to Town, and I will take care that it shall be
safely returned to you. Have you had many visitors
last summer in the steam-vessels at Longstone light?
And have you ever heard from any of the persons
who were saved from the Forfarshire?

With the best wishes of your Guardian, North.[d]

I made a rough draft of an answer, for I still find it a great matter to correspond with a Duke; but he is kind, and I could answer his questions one by one.

My Lord Duke,
I received yours which you honoured me with;
although dated the 11th, it did not arrive here until
the 24th, and beg to return you thanks for the kind
proposal of cleaning my watch, but she still continues
to go well. We have had our Trinity gentlemen

*twice down here this season, in June and Sept., the
first time they brought a barometer and two
thermometers, which is to attend to 4 times in 24
hours, for which I find my watch particularly useful.
We had no pleasure-parties with steam-vessels, but
has had a good many visitors in small parties. The
last were Mr and Mrs Fairleigh of Hough Castle,
which I think to be very good people. After arriving
home they forwarded to me a letter, and a parcel
containing a book of sermons to my Father, and one
to my mother, brother and widowed sister, and
myself; and the North Sunderland boatmen was not
forgot, as they each received one . . .*

'And, my Lord Duke, I shudder to think what they
may have said about such a present as that!' That
thought of course, I did not write.

*We have not heard from any of the persons which
we saved from the wreck of the* Forfarshire. *I have
not got married yet; for they say the man is master,
and there is much talk about bad masters.*

I mused a long while over that last sentence.
Things Thomasin told me of her married customers,
their lives. Things Mary-Ann said; Mary-Ann was
glad enough to be home again. And, my Lord Duke,
what husband am I fit for? Marry a fisherman, and
make of him a rough-mannered, jumped-up gentleman? Be a gentleman's wife, and see the scorn on his
sister's face, his mother's pain at my common birth?
I doubt I could submit to a man who could not read
and think for himself . . . I doubt I could submit to a

man who cannot turn a hand to honest work, who
cannot row or dig, who is timid in danger. Another
like my father will not soon be found. I would be
good for a parson's wife, with all these books of
sermons! But no parson has asked for me save crazy
ones, who ask by letter, never having seen me. I have
my fame to bargain with; shall my husband then
take my name, rather than I his? I did think I might
be an artist's wife . . .

I crossed out the last sentence of the draft, and
replaced it with:

> *I have not got married yet, for I have heard people*
> *say there is luck in leisure.*
> *I have the honour to be, my Lord Duke,*
> *Your most obedient servant . . .*

When I had finished this draft I took it in my
hand to Father, to ask him if he thought it well said.
I found him sitting upon the steps in a patch of
sunshine, working at unknotting a tangled line. He
looked over my letter, and said, 'That is very nice,
Gracie. You had best in your turn look over my
reply to my letter from the Duke. Go and see it; it is
on the pile of papers in the kitchen.'

The pile of Father's letters was near as tall as
mine; it was stacked on the mantelshelf under a
beach pebble for a paperweight. I took off the
pebble, and stood reading Father's unfinished letter:

> *. . . I will endeavour to answer your kind inquiries*
> *in my humble way. We are all very well and Grace*
> *is every way the same girl, and happy in her*

situation; but I should very much like for her to see a little more of the world, but cannot see how it can be done, unless she was to get married, and that she cannot think of for every time she goes on shore she gets a catalogue of this one and the other that has made such a bad job of it. But she is going to write herself . . .

Then I stood thinking a moment. It never does to reckon little of Father's shrewdness; but how did he know about Thomasin's endless gossip? How did he guess what I heard when I went on shore? I had left the door open, and while I stood reflecting a gust of wind blew in and sent Father's papers flying all round the kitchen like falling leaves. I gathered them up. And I glanced at them as I set them in a pile again, putting two- and three-page letters together trying to get them orderly for him. That was how I saw a letter dated London, September 1839, and signed 'J. Reay'. Father had heard from him, many months since, and not even told me!

I read the letter.

Dear Sir,
When I left your hospitable sea-girt dwelling last autumn, I expected I should before this time have had another opportunity of visiting it. In the early part of the year I left home for this great city, intending to stay for about three months. After I arrived here I found that the opportunities for studying my profession were much greater in Paris than here. To France then I immediately set off, and

*there I have been all summer. This I trust will be
some excuse . . .*

My eyes filled with tears, and I barely skimmed the
remaining paragraphs. He had met Mr Joy in Paris,
and was recommending him, sending the letter by
him; Mr Joy had a commission from Lord Panmure
. . . Mr Joy had been and gone months since; this
letter was old.

*It is very probable I will remain here till the winter,
so that I will not have an opportunity of seeing you
this year. I live in hopes of another summer finding
me at home when I will not fail to enjoy myself by
visiting your romantic isle. Will you please remember
me in more than a complimentary way to your
daughters Grace and Thomasin, and all the members
of your family with whom I have the pleasure to be
acquainted?*

I shed bitter tears into my pillow that night. But in
the cold light of a grey dawn, when I kept my
watch I could not conceal from myself the knowledge that it was not so much John Reay's love the
loss of which grieved me, but the loss of that prospect he had held out to me that I might travel with
him, that I might go far, far, away from the lighthouse that had become so crowded, from all that so
disturbed my peace, and see the cities of the world,
compared to which a few zebras in Edinburgh were
a mere nothing!

When some help to me came, it came not from
John Reay, but from the Duke. By and by when

Father and I had each fair-copied our letters and dispatched them, the Duke replied to Father with a brief note. He was pleased with the report Father made of me, that my fame had not changed me. And he thought I might at least have a holiday. If nothing more suitable occurred to us, might I not like to visit my brother on Coquet Island, and give the Duke the pleasure of hearing my opinion on the amenities of his lighthouse there? I could come through Alnwick on my return, and call on him.

Father thought I could not go alone, and so Thomasin was to come with me. Brother William was hugely pleased; and in a flurry of letters and finding schedules for the steam-packets that called at Sunderland, it was all arranged for March – as soon as the days lengthened, but before the trippers resumed their visits in full flood. Neither Thomasin nor I had ever had a holiday.

· 18 ·

There is green grass on Coquet Island. It is about as large as the Brownsman, and one can walk outside every day, in every state of the tide. There are the flocks of birds there at home, and rabbits, against whom my brother and sister-in-law make war in defence of their new garden. The lighthouse being spanking-new was well found and comfortable, with a light and airy kitchen, and a new kind of iron stove, with a roasting oven, a proving oven and a bread oven all set in, and a pair of iron lids over the fire-boxes, to serve as hot plates. You can put a kettle to boil upon the lid, instead of suspended over the fire, getting black with soot. Thomasin and I were much taken with the stove!

William said the Duke himself had said to the Trinity men which sort of stove it ought to be, which gave us all to smile. 'The Duke interests himself in a good deal of fine detail,' William said, 'not only in my sister's doings.'

'Nothing is too much trouble for him,' said Thomasin. 'If it gives occasion to meddle in other people's lives!'

'But, Thomasin, it is an excellent stove,' said Ellen, my sister-in-law, 'much better than the one at Longstone.'

Of course we expected to set to with the work of the household, while we were there. But there was very little to do; only the four of us to cook for, and Thomasin and I had got all their linens and clothes mended in three days, for their things were not badly worn, and Ellen takes good care of everything. William would not have me clean the glass, or oil the machinery, or take a watch, but said he would rather keep in his regular way of things, and not have a big upset with missing our help when we were gone. And so it was like childhood come again, with each day to play with, and fill with harmless doings. I sat for hours in the window, wondering to see Dunstan-borough far north, instead of far south, and my thoughts drifting like the birds on the waves. On the clearest days we could see the Fernes from Coquet, and the Longstone light a pale speck on the horizon in the midday sun. And we could take William's boat, and go to Amble, a little village and harbour on the main, for Coquet is barely a mile offshore. It is easy to come and go.

We crossed often to the mainland, and from Amble walked past Gloster Hill, and wandered along the wooded banks of the River Coquet, hand in hand, and talking idle talk. The trees were in bud of the tenderest green, and the soft leafy floor of the woods was starred with pale wind-flowers, and golden daffodils. The birds sang frantically, their sweet piping songs, so unlike the loud harsh cries of sea-birds, that I wanted to join in – I raised my voice to sing 'Down by the Greenwood sidey, O!' but the catching in my chest stopped me, and turned into coughing, so I left it to the little birds, making a joyful job of it, and the soft sound of the flowing stream accompanying them.

The stream with its clear waters and brown pebbles gave us glimpses of little trout, and I liked its simplicity – flowing one way, as though it knew its mind, not like the endless fretting of the to and fro of the sea. And then to walk at our leisure back, and buy some trifle in the shop at Amble – a card of buttons, or a pot-posy of vegetables – and row ourselves off again to Coquet, where Ellen would have a supper making; no night-dreaming could cast shadows on such pleasant days!

It was a mild and gentle March, but it broke up in stormy weather, and when it was the day appointed for us to leave Coquet, William was concerned for us, and would have had us stay. We could not without much ado, and so he and Ellen brought us on shore to Amble, and parted from us in haste, as it looked set to turn thundery. We had ten miles to walk to Alnwick, and as we went along the road it rained heavily, and we were wet through and chilled in the helm wind, coming off the Pennine ridge, where the snow lay, shining in the sun between storms, beyond the rainbows.

I was bone-cold before we got to Alnwick, and glad to get to Narrowgate, to the MacFarlanes. Our cousins fussed us, and made us tea while we got into dry things – our box had got there that morning – but we were in high spirits, and eager to go about the town and see our friends. Indeed I hoped I might do so before news of our being there got abroad,

and an uproar was occasioned. The Duke and Duchess were departed, a week since, and we were to
make report to Archdeacon Sharp as to how we
found Coquet. I was a little daunted at meeting with
another great personage; but he was very kind. He
gave us a glass of wine apiece, and asked us to come
again on Saturday when he would have a secretary
to write down what we told him.

We were three days in Alnwick, in the end,
before our calling was all done, our friends all seen.
And then home again; the Berwick coach set us
down at Belford, and we walked to Balmboro', and
Saburn brought us off.

It was sweet to be home again, the first evening.
Thomasin came with me, and was to stay till morning,
for there was a pilot boat anchored off the Longstone,
the Admiralty pilots being employed making a new
survey, and the pilot undertook to take her onshore at
daybreak. There was a great clamour at our arrival,
news of William being eagerly sought, and Father was
delighted to see me. He said he had never seen a higher
colour in my cheeks, or my eyes so bright, and praised
Thomasin for her care of me. I had to inspect the
babes' progress, and kiss everyone, and sit down to
rabbit pie, made under a crust all done in cut pastry to
look like one of my medals. There was plans for
Brooks's house to look at, and a mite of news of every
this and that about the lighthouse. Mr Shields had
been with them three days, painting birds, and was
sorry not to have seen us. Everyone made no doubt of
having missed me, and I thought it was so good to be
there again that I should never more leave them.

And yet the next morning, when Thomasin was gone, getting back into the old ways was like putting on clothes again when they are wet. There were so many letters and packets come for me when I was gone that Betsy had put them in a log-basket. I cast around for excuses before starting on them, but of course in my absence Jane and Betsy had shared my work between them, and everything had gone along very nicely without me, and was set so to continue, and I had no family duties to put before the demands of the public, and shelter behind.

For a while I amused myself with Georgian, asking her, 'Where's Aunt Thomasin?'

'Pilot!' she told me, dimpling and smiling. Then I penned a note to Thomasin, to tell her what the child said. Then I unpacked my bag, and put the soiled clothes to soak in a washing-tub, and my outer clothes in my cupboard. And then I was already tired, and coughing a little, and flinching from the sight of the writing-desk and the log-basket full of my tasks. I pulled my little chair up to the window, and rested, with my hands in my lap, looking at the wintry light upon the sea; the grey heaving waters, and the shoals of purple cloud shadows scudding among the white-tops to the horizon. There were three ships on the horizon, when I closed my eyes.

'Gracie was dozing before dinner time, and coughing dreadfully when I woke her,' said Betsy at supper that evening. 'I hope you are well, Gracie.'

'I think I took a chill getting wet on the road to Alnwick,' I said. 'It is nothing.'

'Take it easy, Grace,' Father said. 'Don't get doing things all at once. By and by will be soon enough.'

But when the supper table was cleared, Father asked me to sing for him. 'I have missed your sweet voice, Gracie. Betsy sings like a crow!' he said, and he got down the fiddle from its hook, and struck up 'A North Country Maid', but I disappointed him, for I sang but a few bars before singing started me into coughing, and I had to stop. Betsy and Brooks sang a little; Betsy sings well enough, whatever Father says.

That was a bad chill; I have never quite thrown it off. Since coming back from Coquet, I have never climbed to the lantern without stopping to draw breath at every landing of the stair. Sometimes my own breath burns me in my chest; often I cannot keep from coughing. At night I wake, sweating heavily, my sheets drenched, my bed clammy and comfortless. Night-terrors afflict me; and more and more often the nightmare seeps into my waking mind, and I tremble and panic in broad day. I used to be too busy to have any thoughts but cheerful ones, but times have altered. Now I am as changeable as our North Sea weather.

For an example, I was at my writing, penning a reply to a clergyman who required to know of me what thoughts were uppermost in my mind at the time of the rescue. He was of opinion that the thoughts of those who are engaged in acts of moral beauty will offer spiritual encouragement to others. His was the fourth letter I had answered that day, and I was in perfectly good spirits as I commenced to write to him.

. . . at the time I believe I had very little thought of
anything but to exert myself to the utmost, my spirit
was so worked up by the sight of such a dreadful
affair, that I can imagine I still see the sea flying
over the vessel . . .

and as I wrote this, panic overwhelmed me. I had no
thoughts of moral beauty to offer. I could not remember what I had thought. *I could not remember
thinking!* But how then could I know I had not
been thinking about money – how could I know
the nightmare was not the plain truth – I had got
up, I had looked through the window, I had seen
money clinging to the rock . . .

I tried to take a hold on myself. Plain sense was
once my strength! Come, Grace, remember carefully,
step by step. I said, 'Can we get them, Father?' He said,
'We might if Brooks were here.' I said, 'I must take
Brooks's oar . . .' He explained the risk to me, while he
laced his boots. We never thought of, we never
mentioned money! I am safe! No cormorant girl! But
with the flood of relief came creeping another memory;
Father *did* mention money! Didn't he speak of the
premiums, as we struggled to put the coble in the
water? What did he say? *I can't remember!*

Just then Betsy came up to the bedchamber.
'There is tea making, Grace, and Jane has baked
parkin. Will you come down?' Then she saw me
looking offish.

'Why, you are trembling, Grace. Is it the coughing? Let me bring some tea up to you.'

When she had brought it and gone, I thought, 'I cannot remember what Father said. But I could look what he wrote!' I went down one flight of stairs, going quietly, into Father and Mother's room, and I did what I had never done before, never dreamed of doing. I took Father's journal down from the shelf, and read in it.

It was most terse and brief. So little did Father write that all the years of my life were between my hands, in this one volume. I turned rapidly through the years – there was no entry at all for some of them – and found the 7th September, 1838. It was headed,

'MELANCHOLY'

Sept' 5. The steam boat Forfarshire, *400 tons sailed from Hull for Dundee on the sixth, at midnight. When off Berwick, her boilers became so leaky as to render the engine useless. Captain Humble then bore away for Shields, blowing strong gale, north, with thick fog. About 4 a.m. on the 7th, the vessel struck the west point of Harker Rock, and in fifteen minutes broke through by the paddle-axle, and drowned forty-three persons, nine having previously left in their own boat and were picked up by a Montrose vessel, and carried to Shields, and nine others held on by the wreck and were rescued by the Darlings. The cargo consisted of superfine cloths, hardware, soap, boiler plate and spinning-gear.*

I could not make sense of this entry. I thought at first Father had not mentioned my part at all; then I thought that perhaps when he wrote 'nine others were rescued by the Darlings', he meant by himself and me, not simply as I had first thought, 'rescued by the lighthouse coble', for our coble was called *The Darlings*.

So I began to turn his pages to and fro, looking for how he had written other things, to see how to understand his words.

There was a great catalogue of shipwrecks, dating from before I was born. And lists of sea-birds taken, and spars and such salvaged. Visits of the Trinity boat, notes of the storms, of a year when there was snow, and the ice was eight inches thick on the Brownsman pond.

I began to skim rapidly: '... *this summer earwigs very numerous in the garden ... two tremendous gales ... the garden small seeds being all above the ground were totally blown off or destroyed ... this year corn very high; flour 6s 3d, oatmeal 4s 8d ...*' Then I thought to look back how he had entered the loss of the *Autumn*, which had given us so much excitement that Christmas.

December 27th. Wind S. by E. fresh gale. 11p.m. the sloop Autumn *of and to Peterhead, with coals from Sunderland struck east point of Knavestone and immediately sank. Crew of three men; two lost, one saved by the lightkeeper, and three sons, viz. William, Robert and George, after a struggle of three hours. Having lost two oars on the rock had a very narrow escape ...*

When I saw my brothers' names I looked again at

the entry Father made for the loss of the *Forfarshire*, and found again no mention of mine. I had not read it quite all the first time, for under a heading 'Forfarshire *further particulars*' he had made note of the coming out of the Sunderland boat. I felt myself lost, like a boat in a sea fret, not knowing which way is land. I felt grief for myself, a person missing, a person lost from view. So for a few moments more I looked for myself. I turned back and back, and found 1815, the year of my birth. There was nothing entered for the 24th November, but for the 25th November there was written, '*Mr James Blackett, myself and T. Fender caught four old seals in waterhole, middle of Northernhairs.*' I could just glimpse myself then, as I could glimpse myself in '*rescued by the Darlings*' which might have meant me, and might have meant the boat; Dr Fender had attended my mother for my birth in Balmboro', as I had often heard tell; if he came seal-hunting with Father on the islands the day after I was born, perhaps he and Mr Blackett had brought news of me. As for seeking to know what I was thinking of when I did any deed, no use to ask Father's journal, for I am off the margins of his page; my thoughts if I cannot remember them are lost, sunk deep as a wreck in the shifting tides.

And with these reflections came a whispering in my head. 'What you will not remember waking comes to you in sleep; how you filched the money from your brother and his bullies . . .'

Father was standing in the door. He came across to me, and took the book from my hands, and closed it and put it on the shelf again. He said, 'You are not well. Go to your bed, and I will bring you a tot of rum.'

'I said it is nothing, Father. Only that I cannot throw off this cold.'

He said, 'I will fetch out Doctor Fender. I don't like to hear you coughing like your poor brother.'

As he turned to leave me, I said, 'Father, why did we do it?'

'Because we were able,' he said, looking at me with that bright gaze he has, his head cocked slightly as he stared. 'If it were to do again, you would do it again, would you not? Or would you leave the poor souls standing there, and spare us all the fuss? Well, Grace?'

'Well, Father!' I said, and he smiled at me, and patted my arm gently as he left.

· 19 ·

I was in my bed three days, with our daily visitors all disappointed of even a glimpse of me, but after that I was better somewhat, and on my feet again. It seemed to me a great fuss everyone made around me, Father mentioning my brother Job, who died ten years since; Father fetching the doctor out here in rough weather, only to look at a chill. Doctor Fender had done me no service. He had told everyone that I must have quiet, that I must exert myself as little as possible. My family had questioned him closely, and he gave answers which burdened me heavily. The company of the babes, he thought, I should have little of; the household tasks should be taken from me. But he thought I might answer letters without harm to my health, and receive visitors, if I did so sitting down.

So for these past many months I could never be busy. A visitor who finds me in a chair lingers, gawping and talking; one who found me cleaning carbon-black, or mending clothes, would seldom detain me long. And those letters! How long ago was it Father told me this must soon die down? Latterly they are mostly from clergymen. They are full of church language, but what they want of me is to know my thoughts. I know well we were close to God when we set out in towering seas to the wreck of the *Forfarshire*; any minute we might have gone for ever to our maker, we were so close! But my thoughts were of matters like the pull of the tide. I can offer no enlightenment to these men of God; I would rather have thought they might offer some to me.

More than once I have had to attend at Balmboro' Castle where a number of men of the cloth wished to talk with me, as Mr Smeddle's guests. On the last occasion Archdeacon Sharp was there. Mr Smeddle gives me hen-flesh now, he so defers to me! Whenever he introduces me he names me the Duke's ward; but it is worse by far when he joins with his guests in asking my opinion of some church matter!

'Do you believe in justification by works?' one of these grand men of the cloth asked me. I said that I believed work was my justification. When I have been on shore, sometimes, I told them, I have observed people sitting down in the evening, and playing at cards or suchlike, saying that their work was done; but I have never known a waking moment when my work was done, and finishing one task means simply taking up another. I trust my Saviour is pleased with me for working, but that it could not be for everyone. 'Why not?' they all asked. 'Because, then how would the gentry stand at the gate of heaven?' said I.

'Out of the mouths of babes . . .' said someone.

Another of these solemn gentlemen then warned me very heavily of the dangers of my new great wealth. Those words about it being hard for a rich man to enter the gates of heaven now applied to me! Secretly, I rejoiced at my knowledge that I should never spend it, but meanwhile they were explaining to me that they meant 'justification by *works*', not by work; in contradistinction to justification by faith.

Then they began to discuss amongst themselves, very eagerly, a story about a doctor who healed a man of a sickness, not because he wished to relieve suffering, but so that the man might live long enough to give him, the doctor, a certain silver cup.

'Although healing is a good act in itself, you will not say in such a case, there could be any merit in it?'

'There might seem to have been merit in the deed, to the sick man, and to all the onlookers,' someone said, 'but in the eyes of God who knows the secrets of every heart, there could be none.'

On that they seemed agreed. 'What made your deed holy in the eyes of God, Miss Darling, was that pure and perfect compassion for suffering humanity that impelled you to launch your frail vessel upon the storm . . .'

'Ah, in the compassionate emotions womanhood has so much to teach, mankind so much to learn!' said another, shaking his head.

'Come, Mr Smeddle,' said Archdeacon Sharp, 'Miss Darling looks pale. Shall we not offer her some refreshment?' So then the housekeeper took me away, and we had a little spiteful talk together about the airy notions of the clergy, that made me smile.

'What they may know about works that couldn't do a good day's work to save their souls, I'll never know!' she said to me. 'Not like you and me, Miss Darling. I know that I work honestly enough; and you, they tell me, have worked yourself into a cough. You must take better care, my dear. Your sister was worried when last I spoke with her.'

'Thomasin? How does she hear I am not well?'

'Why, all the trippers bring reports of your pallor, and your cough, my dear.'

'But you see for yourself, Mrs Partle, you must tell her I am well.'

'It would better come direct from you, I think. Now what do you say to a slice of my Madeira cake, and a glass of porter?'

I said yes to both, before going up the street to find Thomasin, and set her mind at rest. But since she was from home, and I had to catch a favourable turn of tide, I had need to write to her.

I wrote her our little news; we had had the Trinity men to see us. They had come to see all was well with the building of Brooks's new house, and they had brought new kitchen fireplaces for us, and for Mr Smith on Inner Ferne, and they were the same as the Coquet one, which much pleased us. The light-keepers got new suits, all blue. The trousers were braided down the sides, and the coats were long-tailed, with splendid buttons. They were all very kind, and offered to take presents and messages to Coquet, where they were going next. I wrote how young Billy was unwell, and Jane would get him to the doctor; Mother was tired, but better this week.

We were troubled by the noise of the masons working on the footings for Brooks's house. Georgian had a pink dress, but we did not know who it was from. Brooks thought it was the woman who sold laces and ribbons in Sunderland, but she had come to the boat and thrown the dress down, and said it was for Georgian, and that was all we knew about it. No news but the best! I wrote to her.

I hoped to set her mind at rest. She is much concerned about me; Thomasin is very ready to be angry, and now she is angry at the world for harassing me. She would have us turn all the visitors away, refuse all invitations, never mind offending. She fears what all the uproar may do to my health and calm. And I know well enough that my health is marred by constant coughing, and my calm vanished long ago, but still I would not have her fret about me. No use for both of us to fret.

But I have sleepless nights on top of thronged and busy days. Can it be true that in the eyes of God who sees our secret thoughts, saving life could be an act with no merit in it, if it were done for the wrong reason – for a wicked reason, like desire for the gift of a silver cup? Was that what the learned clergymen at the castle had been saying? In that case, if I had indeed done my deed for money, then all the presents, all the praise and love I had been given had been given in error, taken on false pretences. I would cough, and toss and turn, and wrestle with thoughts like these. No doubt John Reay had seen through me to my wicked heart, and that is why he had not come again . . .

Yet all this while I knew, as though lost somewhere within me a ghost of myself still knew, that what tormented me was moonshine, only that I could barely hear the voice.

One thing I had in plenty was books of sermons. I looked in them for some information, about whether good deeds were turned to wicked ones by bad reasons, but I could find nothing on the matter save that the secrets of our hearts were most weighty in finding out our merits. And the more I sought to remember the less I could remember. I could not remember why I had offered to take Brooks's oar. Perhaps for the love of strangers, and pity for their state; perhaps for the love of the premiums, or the hope of glory – the truth was I could remember not a thought about it other than whether, there being only Father and me, it could be done.

Father kept reaching out a hand to me, touching my forehead to feel if I were warm or no; whenever I entered the kitchen I found the chair nearest the fire left empty for me; Mother made me custards and gruel, and spoke softly to me. If she and I were alone in the room a moment, she would sing softly the old tunes that came from her childhood to ours:

> *'Where hesta' bin, maw bonny bairn,*
> *Where hesta bin, maw canny hinny? . . .'*

So had she soothed me of baby ailments, long ago.

Jane tried to hush the babes when they were near me, though I loved their cheerful din.

And I grew even sadder as those around me grew so kind. I had been happier to be endlessly useful, and little regarded. I thought I might contrive to go onshore and see the parson at Balmboro', and ask him what he thought about good deeds and secret reasons. He it was who was our appointed shepherd over our souls, not all those clergymen from Durham I had met before. Alnwick was too far, Archdeacon Sharp too grand for me.

I could not think of a reason to ask to go on the main, but in the end I was sent, not for the parson but for the doctor. One of our crowds of trippers, stopping upon the threshold as he took his leave, said to his companion, 'It is consumption the poor girl has; plain as daylight!' And Father heard him.

Then in a fright he called out Dr Fender once again. I was sure he would say it was but a lingering chill. But the doctor pulled a long face when he had listened carefully to my breathing, and told Father I should go onshore. 'Between the close confinement of your rooms in bad weather, and the rough breezes of the open sea outside your door, it is not healthy here,' he said.

'I have always thought it is a harsh, but a health-giving life,' said Father.

'Not for such a condition as your daughter has,' the doctor said. He waited while Mother, fretting and lamenting, made up a bag for me, stuffing it full of little packets of tea and sugar, and gingerbread, and camomile lotion, and suchlike, and got me ready to go to Thomasin.

'The air is better, softer, on the main,' Dr Fender said. 'I shall be at hand, rain or shine, and she can be coddled by her sister.' Brooks rowed me over; and I faced the sweep of the mainland, as it seems to curve round our wide bay, and all the islands. But I looked often over my shoulder at the dark rocks, and the white tower, at the pinnacles topped with guano, and the flocks of birds that fanned their wings in the breezes, at the ruined tower on the Brownsman, and the circuit of the walls round our garden; only the other day we had worked till sunset there, and seen the whole spectacle of our vistas turn with sunset to crimson and vermilion. Then at the house and light on Inner Ferne, and the ruins of Cuthbert's Chapel as we passed it and crossed the Sound – I looked as long as I could on all these things. And there was a great stillness and sadness in my heart, as if I would never see the well-loved, sea-washed wilderness again.

Brooks took my bag to Thomasin's door for me, with a sombre face on him, and kissed me as tenderly as a lover when he left me, but once she opened the door I was joyful again and giddy. 'We shall have holiday again, sister!' I said to her. 'I am sent to you for being sick, and I am quite well, and we shall be snug and happy together!'

'Sit down while I mend the fire,' she said. 'Oh, but Gracie, you are dwining; you look thin!'

'No, no,' I said, 'I am nearly quite well. As I wrote to you, it is no news but the best!'

And yet I was very sorry to be parted from the babes. I have come to love the babes extremely, and to lean on them for comfort, because they neither admire me nor resent me, but in their innocent selfishness make good use of me, getting from me rhymes and games and comfits, and the names of birds, and playing peek-a-boo in the folds of my skirt, until almost I can remember who I am.

· 20 ·

We were quiet together at Balmboro'. Thomasin sat one side of the fire, at her sewing, and I the other, sometimes lending a hand at a simple hem, or at tacking stitches. I had brought my knitting with me, but often it lay unattended in my lap. Sometimes if I felt well enough we walked to the foot of the street and up again, in a mild summer afternoon. Dr Fender came often, with advice about what I must eat, and with medicine for me. Friends called on us; Father came once or twice. Slowly I grew familiar with the sounds of the shore; with the changing colour of the trees as they deepened from spring to summer shades, with the song of garden birds, and the sound of a high wind in the house eaves, and with the silence of the little house at night, where no machinery slowly turned, and the darkness lay undisturbed over us like a thick blanket, and now and then we heard an owl hooting in the elm trees, threatening some tiny squeaking beastie.

I pined a little for home. In the long mild evenings I could cross the road, and walk into the churchyard, and go past my grandparents' headstone, and that of the Reverend Robb, who had died upon Harker Rock before Father and I got there. The poor gentleman had been much loved, and there were eloquent sad words upon his slab. Further down, if I walked right to the lower wall of the sloping churchyard, it was possible to see the tip of the Fernes, just the Longstone itself. From anywhere nearer, from anywhere else in the churchyard or the town, one cannot see them, because the church, and the great bulk of the castle on its prominence, come between. I liked it most to go down there and look out at dusk, when everything is wrapped in softness, and the Longstone light is put up; I loved to see it far away in the veils of evening, a blazing and then fading flash, as the reflectors turned, and the count of thirty between one peak of brightness and the next. I would take out my famous watch, and time the interval, as though it were still for me to mind it. And if it shone out, and the count was precise I felt as though all in the world was well. I cannot tell if Father knew how every evening I checked the lantern from afar, though perhaps he did, for Thomasin scolded me about it, and no doubt complained to him.

As she complained bitterly to people in Balmboro' who told visitors where I was to be found, so that they came calling at Thomasin's house for me, or stood outside in the road, gawping at the windows. Soon our good friends and neighbours kept mum, and our visitors became so few as to be bearable. Mr Smeddle came, and his wife, bringing jellies from the castle kitchen, and a parcel of advice, which agreed not with the doctor's.

And the parson came. It was the new parson – the Reverend Darnell, who had come to Balmboro' just last year. He was a young man – after so many years of Parson Bolt, who had been with us forty years, Mr Darnell seemed too young to be a parson. He cannot have been as old as my brother William. But he was, of course, a man of God. He asked me if there were anything he might do for me, and I told him he might, if he would, set my mind at rest upon a matter of conscience.

'I would be glad to help with any little problem,' he said. 'What is it?'

'I need to know,' I said, 'if it is true that a good deed might be changed into a wicked one if done for bad reasons.'

'Why, who has put such matters as that into your head, Miss Darling?' he said, seeming much surprised.

'Archdeacon Sharp and his friends.'

'But was such a question *directed* at you, or did you merely overhear it?'

'I am not entirely sure. I was a part of the conversation.'

'It is true that theologians – learned men of the Church – would hold that the nature of a deed is affected by motives. That is why we are warned to do acts of charity in secret, lest they be changed into acts of vainglory. But, my dear Miss Darling, this is – how shall I put it? – this is an arcane point; not to do with everyday conduct. You should not trouble yourself about it. It was intended as a warning to princes, and great men. It was not to apply to a person like yourself living a simple and virtuous life.'

'But does it not apply to me?' I asked him, getting agitated. 'Have you not heard talk about me, how greed and avarice were my reasons for what I did?'

He hesitated, so that I saw at once that he knew what the rumour was.

Then he said, 'If I heard talk such as that, it is not your motives I would be suspicious of, Miss Darling, but those of the speaker.'

'But what if I told you that I feared it was quite true?'

'I should say it was your illness speaking to me; I should ask your sister to make you a hot posset, and read to you till bedtime from a cheerful book.'

'Can I not then commit a fault like anyone else? Why do you think not? Am I not flesh and blood like other young women?'

He looked at me gravely. 'Of course you are. And it is not uncommon for young women to torment themselves on fine matters of conscience. Often they are kept in such idleness it is all they have to think about. But, Miss Darling, I am a parson. I have a lot to do with sinners, and I know a good deal about them. Believe me, you are not much like a sinner, more like a sensible young woman who has become ill. If you were not an honest good girl, the attentions which have been lavished on you would sooner have made you think yourself perfect, than sinful, I believe.'

'When people ask me what was in my heart that morning, I find that I cannot remember.'

'Why think the worst of yourself then? I will tell you what you must have thought: that as your

Saviour, Christ Jesus, suffered and died for you, you would now risk death for love of him, knowing that he requested us to love one another, that your brothers and sisters in Christ were exposed in imminent danger of death, and that he promised us that he who lost his life should save it. Is this not perfectly likely? Now I shall ask your sister about that hot posset. And I shall pray for you.'

So I thanked him, with a heavy heart. For no such sermon thoughts as those could possibly have been in my head, and I knew it.

That night I dreamed again worse than ever. It was silver upon the rock — thirty silver coins, and they were fouled with blood. I stood precariously in the gale, perched upon the edge of Harker Rock, and washed the money in the flying spray, and put it in my purse. Then I thought, 'It is not mine, I must give it to Brooks,' and I tried to give it to him, but the coins stuck to my fingers, and would not be let go. I woke crying, and Thomasin came in her nightgown to comfort me. She showed me a letter from Mr Shields at Wooler, inviting us to go and stay with him and his family, and try if mountain air would suit me better than the air of the coast.

'I would love to take us to him, Grace, if you were well enough,' she said. 'He is so kind. And we would be quite safe from any visitors at all — nobody would find us there. But I must send him an answer no.'

'Send him yes, Thomasin,' I said. 'I would like to see a new place. And I feel so much better; I am perfectly well enough.'

'Since when do you feel better, sister?' she asked.

'Since you came in with your candle,' I said, smiling. 'But let us go to Wooler, Thomasin.'

· 21 ·

The air was sweet at Wooler. It came from the high Cheviot clear and pure, and not a breath of salt sea about it. There was fine weather, with a warmth that lingered into the evenings as it never did about the lighthouse. Mr Shields's garden was sheltered, and full of roses, with a few late lilies whose sweetness filled the air around them, and drew purring insects from far and wide. Mr Shields's wife and daughters made us welcome, gave over a room to us with a prospect down the garden and towards the town. Thomasin had nothing to do, for the Shields family ran around after my every need, and made a great ado over making things for me to eat. When I had been there a week I felt quite recovered, and on Mr Shields asking if there was anything I was missing, I answered, only the sight of the Fernes.

'That you shall have! This very day — I do believe you are well enough!' he said, and he put the whole household in an uproar, making a picnic lunch, and making ready a cart, to take us to the hills. Then so many of us wished to come that the cart would not take us all, and I begged to be allowed the use of the little pony. We were all gone off to the hills by about ten-thirty, and I rode the distance of five miles on the pony, all the way, sometimes going before, and sometimes behind the cart. We went as far as the Common Burn, and went into one of the hinds' houses, where a kindly woman welcomed us, and gave us milk to drink.

'Build your strength, peaky lassie; have another ladle full,' she said to me, refilling my cup.

'Do you know who this is?' Mr Shields asked her. 'This is Miss Darling; Grace Darling of Longstone Light.'

The woman made me a slight curtsy, but looked at me so blankly that I knew she had never heard of me. That made me glad. A little beyond the hind's house, our party divided. Mr Shields maintained he had kept his promise to me of a sight of home, for we were high enough now that we could see far away, on the rim of the world it seemed, the sea shining beyond the land; and just make out, with the help of Mr Shields's spy-glass – he has it for birds, being a keen painter of birds – a string of purple specks in the silver light of the waters, which Mr Shields assured me were my homelands, the Ferne Islands. And when I put his spy-glass to my eye I could just make out the Longstone tower, a tiny streak of white, and I laughed for pleasure at the sight.

The promise being kept, Mr Shields advised me to go home, and not allow myself to get tired out, but Mr Thompson, a Shields cousin, and Thomasin and the two Shields daughters were wishful to go further, and they went on foot, taking the pony that they might ride by turns, saying they would be on top of the Cheviot, before they turned back. Mr Shields and I were home easily by about three o'clock, and I went to rest; but the others came not back till about half past nine, the lamps being already lit, and the sunset over. They came very tired, and full of delight, having got half-way up the Cheviot, and had the pleasure of fine views – better than those we had seen, they boasted, and had seen vipers, they said, and gathered clumps of wild thyme to plant in the garden paths.

'What a day!' Mr Shields cried. 'What an excellent day! Now supper at once, and bed for every tired walker! I can't tell you, my dear,' he said, turning to me, 'how it warms my heart to see you looking so well and beautiful!'

'I do feel better,' I told him. 'But fie, Mr Shields, I have never been beautiful!'

'Come, my dear,' he said, and taking me by the hand he led me to look in the gilded mirror framed over the mantelpiece. I saw myself in the lamplight. I was as pale as any lady that never laboured in the sunlight. But there was a bright patch of high colour in my cheeks. My face had thinned and fined, so that the bones shaped through, and my eyes were very large and glassy-dark, so that I thought I might see tiny fishes and anemones in them, like brown rockpools.

'I shall be plain again in the morning!' I said, and everyone laughed.

I did not look again in the mirror the next morning, the first of September, still keeping fair and warm. But a letter came from cousins John and Ann

MacFarlane in Alnwick. They said they had so many inquiries after my health, from both rich and poor, that they must have news from us. They said the Queen had sailed past to Edinburgh, and was expected in Alnwick on her return journey. The Duke and Duchess were to come back to meet her; their horses and luggage were already come. They wrote if we had any desire to see the Queen, their house was a home to us.

'Could we go without there being an affray?' asked Thomasin.

'Why, everyone will be looking at the Queen,' I said. 'There will be no thought to spare for me!'

Mr Shields did not think it wise, and would be sorry to part from us; but I wanted to see the Queen, and I felt well and cheerful, and so we wrote to Father, to ask his opinion of a plan to go to Alnwick.

Father wrote:

Our dear Daughters,
We received both your letters yesterday as the
weather was bad on Monday, and the boat did not
get here. The news they contained was not so good as
we could have wished, but should you be certain of
your strength increasing I have no fears for the
cough . . .

Thomasin must have told him in her letter that I still coughed; which was true, but I would have kept from him.

As you have given Wooler a fair trial I think

233

your plan is good in going to Alnwick. To give you
time to be there I think I will not start from here
until Monday next the 19th, inst. and if you possibly
can, be there beforehand.

As I hope to see you soon I will not bother with
writing much only that we are all well and Georgian
and Billy are grown two noisy fellows. He is now
nearly quite better and can walk between, with hold
of a finger or two. Since they got the stones from
Warren the work is going on better — Brooks's house
is right for the window sills. I must go to the
barometer.

Our kind love to you both. Wm. Darling.

This letter made my heart ache. It brought to my
mind's eye so clearly what I missed — the children
growing, and Father tenderly giving his fingers as a
walking-stick — he must have needed to stoop to that,
tall as he is — I should like to have seen that! — and
the work of the lighthouse going forward through
the day, the barometer at certain hours, the weather
reports at others. No one could be kinder than Mr
Shields, but I could not wait but to be nearer home,
near enough for Father to visit, as he would at Alnwick. Nor, with Father's letter at hand, would Mr
Shields oppose it, though he gave Thomasin a great
sermon full of instructions about how she was to
keep me quiet, keep me obedient to the doctor in
Alnwick, turn away visitors, and so and so on. Thus
beaten about the ears by his affection, we left for
Alnwick.

· *22* ·

The journey set me back. Our cousins made us welcome, and gave us a little upstairs room for our own, quite comfortable, though dark, for the house is overshadowed by the castle walls. I did not quite see the Queen, though I saw her carriage pass below the window, where my kind cousins had placed me in a chair. I heard the crowds roar for her, and saw them waving flags. Thomasin, who was below in the street, caught a glim at her.

Mr Shields pursued us with letters, imploring me to heed the advice of the doctor who had been called to see me by John MacFarlane, rejoicing to learn that this doctor had been so kind as to order me to be kept quiet. *'My dear friend,'* he wrote, *'insist upon it. Nothing can do more injury to you than visitors to put you about.'*

But how could I insist? The MacFarlanes had many friends, and customers they could not well afford to offend; and though they did their best, their little house was full of coming and going, and people paying calls. Mr Shields threatened to scold and punish Thomasin, the old maid, my nurse, for any neglect of me; he might tease and cajole all he would, and she do all she could, still I was weak and fretful, and coughing all night, and longing for Father to come.

When Father did come he kissed me, and looked round our room. He put his carpet-bag upon the floor, and changed his old jacket for his new one, with the fine buttons, and the long tails, and said he was going to call upon the Duke.

'One cannot call upon the Duke without arrangement, cousin!' said John MacFarlane.

'I can, and will,' Father said.

'You can call as a courtesy. You will not see the Duke himself,' said Ann MacFarlane.

But when Father came again he told us he had been taken directly to the Duke himself. Father told us the Duke was most distressed to learn that I was ill. He had said that lodging in Narrowgate with the main traffic of the town going past the doors would not do at all; he had said his own physician, Dr Barnfather, should be sent to me at once; he had called the Duchess into the room, and told her with tears in his eyes that his Ward was sick, and she had promised every little comfort for me that skill and devotion could devise . . .

'God knows we have done our best for her!' said John MacFarlane. 'But it is true that the most we can do is easily surpassed by the least trouble taken by a Duke!'

'I know you have done all you can,' Father said. 'But look at my poor child, John. Could you blame me for reaching out for any help for her that may be to be had?'

And I said, 'But, Father, I am not really ill. Only

that the cough deprives me of sleep, and leaves me weary. I shall soon be better and come home.'

'Please God, Gracie,' he said.

Father could not stay long. And by the next midday the Duke's servants had come for us, with his carriage, and taken us to a little house in the upper part of the town, called Green Bat, on Prudhoe Street. It was a gentleman's house, with high ceilings and airy rooms, and the windows facing south across the churchyard, towards the sun. The rooms were full of pretty furniture, and flowers from the castle gardens, and our bedrooms, which had a door between, had lace-trimmed linens on the beds, and dressing-tables with bowls of pomanders sweetly spicing the air, and carpets on the floors.

For a while we went from room to room – I leant on Thomasin's arm – exclaiming in pleasure at these luxuries, astonished that such apartments should be ours, and choosing which room should be mine, and which hers, and laughing, trying the chairs in the pretty sitting-room. We had supposed ourselves alone, and we were even more astonished to find in the kitchens of the house a young maid-servant in uniform. She told us that the Duchess had sent her to keep the house clean, and run errands for us, because Miss Thomasin would have enough to do nursing me.

'Show me then where things are in the kitchen,' said Thomasin, and the girl said there was no need; she would make tea and hot possets for us, and our meals were all to be sent from the castle kitchens.

'What is your name?' I asked her.

'Sarah,' she said.

'Well, Sarah, we have never had a servant before, and the work of the house has been for us to do. You must tell us how to use you, and scold us if we get it wrong!' I said. 'It must be a downcoming for you to be sent to wait on us instead of a Duchess!'

Sarah said, 'It is very easy, Miss Grace. You look after yourself, and I look after the tea-kettles and the brooms.'

'Could we have some tea very soon?' I asked her.

'The doctor will be here soon, Miss Grace,' she said. 'He would be pleased to find you settled, I think. I will bring tea to the sitting-room.'

'But my dear sister!' said Thomasin, once we were comfortably sitting down. 'What will we do all day?'

Doctor Barnfather, when he came, most sternly directed I should do nothing. There should be no visitors except my family and dearest friends, and they should leave in a quarter hour or so, no longer. I should write no letters at all to any person in the general public, but send everything of that nature to the Duke's secretaries for reply. He made a prescription for medicines to be got from the apothecary, and he made a list of what I might and might not eat. Finally he said I was on no account to go out of doors while the wind was blowing from the sea. Sea air, he said, had done me injury and must be avoided.

Father was holed up at Sunderland, and could not get home because of the storms, and while he was there he wanted to hear from us every day after dinner, at least three lines each. He gave us an account of a shipwreck – a boatload of stone for Brooks's house had gone down, and the survivors left standing for hours, but were saved by a fishing-smack. He had got a hamper of apples sent from John MacFarlane, and as he had not paid for it we were to make it up to him. Cousin Ann had sent a doll and a flute for the babes. His letter made us smile, for it was addressed 'To Grace and Governess' and indeed Thomasin deserved the title, for she ordered me about without mercy.

We were no good at doing nothing. Both at Wooler, and with our cousins in Narrowgate, we had turned our hands to little tasks. Even in my weariness I could sit mending a sock, or rubbing the tarnish off flatware. Now we were quite idle, and so bad at bearing it that after a day Thomasin went out and bought some fine muslin, and cut out a dress for Georgian, and some handkerchiefs for us to hem. We would both begin after breakfast, and I would work a little, and then drowse. I would get a fit of coughing, and wake to find Thomasin nearly finished her hemming, and mine scarce begun. She scolded me for pricking my fingers, and specking the work with blood, which she held to be very poor workmanship, but I thought I had not done, only that she was right about the speckles.

The Duchess and her niece came calling on us, and frightened us very much with their rustling silks, and their fluttering fans, and close questioned us about everything we were doing. I knew not what to say to her, so I told her Father's story about the recent wreck. She seemed more curious about my cough.

'Your father is gone back to the Longstone?' she asked us.

'Yes, Your Grace. The weather detained him in Sunderland some time, but he is gone now, for our last letters to him at Sunderland were returned to us. The weather is very bad, and we shall not have any news from the Longstone till it is calmer.'

'It cannot be pleasant being cut off from your family. You must let us supply any wants,' said the Duchess.

'Our friend Mr George Shields from Wooler has been to see us, and our cousins run errands for us,' said Thomasin fiercely.

'Of course you have many friends and admirers,' said the Duchess, looking hard at Thomasin. 'I meant only to refer to anything great or small which we might the most easily afford to you. Is Doctor Barnfather looking after you well?'

'He is very kind.'

'And you are doing exactly as he says?'

'Yes, indeed.'

'I am sure he has directed you that your visits should be kept short,' she said, rising to go.

The hardest of Doctor Barnfather's directions was that I should keep indoors. There was a soft fine Sunday when I so longed to go out and walk upon the pavement outside the house, or go into the churchyard, that I implored Thomasin to let me.

'Only for a few minutes, sister; just enough to fill my lungs with open air! Be kind; allow me!'

But Thomasin would not. She could not, she said; Doctor Barnfather had forbidden it, and she knew not what effects the medicine he was giving me might have; she could not risk us judging for ourselves if the walk might do good or no.

'But sister, I feel so much better, and a little walk will just set me up.'

The most she would undertake was to ask the doctor when he came next, if I might go out for a few moments in fine weather. But she did not ask Doctor Barnfather in my hearing, and it happened that Mr Shields had called to see us, and was in the house when the doctor came. When the doctor had sounded my chest, and taken my pulse, and talked to me a little, he went into the parlour downstairs, and talked a long time with Mr Shields behind closed doors. Then he came again to me, and said things were going along as he expected, and his medicine was working as he had expected, and to continue just as before. Thomasin followed him down the stairs, and I heard her then asking about going out, and if she might let me walk on the pavement in front of the house for a few steps if it should again be as fine as it had been last Sunday.

'She seems so bright and cheerful, and is so eager to step outside,' Thomasin was telling him.

I got up, and though I walked but shakily, I crept to the head of the stair, and leaned over the banister to overhear them talking below. Sarah was at the door, holding the doctor's hat and stick, and she looked up and saw me, but I laid my finger on my lips in sign to her, and she did not betray me.

'Alas! you cannot count on how she feels, Miss Darling,' the doctor was saying gravely. 'This is *spes phthisica*, or in plain words, "the hope of the consumptive". At the very door of death patients with your sister's condition make plans to travel, to marry, to plant gardens, to write books. The disease brings moods of elation, varied with moods of despair, and often the patient refuses to think himself ill at all, and makes light of all his suffering.'

'At the door of death!' cried Thomasin. 'Oh, say not so, sir . . .'

'God willing, she is not. And in any case not yet. You must with iron determination know better than she does how ill she may be. Keep her indoors, and warm and quiet at all times.'

And I thought, 'What a fuss they are all making about this pestilential cough of mine! I must throw it off quickly, or they will be ordering me about like this all winter!' Then, as the door closed on the doctor the banister twisted, and pulled out of my hand, and the floor of the landing tilted up like a boat on a wave, and struck me. Then I was lying on the carpet, and they were all running up the stairs towards me. I was lifted into bed. I saw that Mr Shields was crying silently – the tears flowed down his cheeks. He said to Thomasin that he would write to Father, and she said she would write also.

'And me,' I said. 'I must write too!' But when Thomasin brought me pen and paper I had no strength for it. I wrote,

Dear Mother and Father,

*As I cannot write you a long letter this time, please
God in a little time I will write a long one. I am
your loving daughter, Grace H. Darling.*

Thomasin folded it in with hers.

There followed a dreadful day, with a cold sleet
beating hard upon our windows, so that we were
happy to be indoors. I stirred not from my bed, and
we were surprised when letters were brought to us
from the lighthouse. It was Mary-Ann who wrote,
full of news of the doings at home, the going on of
Brooks's house, and news of Georgian. Thomasin
read it to me:

*'Georgian is learning to talk very well; she says
"Mammy, me better go in coble-boatty, see my Grace
and make her better, and give her tea and cuddle
her." She often sits down to write letters to you with
a little nail.* Then she asked for three pairs of
stockings for Georgian, and then, *Mother is
thinking of going to see you but is afraid of the
journey, please don't neglect to write often.
With love to you both, Mary-Ann.'*

This letter filled my eyes with tears. Thomasin said,
'Oh, what's amiss, Gracie?' and I told her I was
longing to see Georgian, and get that cuddle from
her. 'Everyone loves me so much, Thomasin, it
would be very wicked of me not to get better!'

'Indeed it would, Grace,' she said hoarsely. 'See to
it, will you!'

And then there was a bustle in the hall, and the Duchess had come. She came to my bedside, her niece beside her, and stood over me, all lace and finery, and asked how I was, and I was so tired, that I could hardly answer her. It seemed to me that my breathing was riding rough over my words, and I could not get them out.

She stayed only a moment or two. I heard her say to Thomasin outside the bedroom door, 'I am distressed at the change in her. She can hardly speak.'

And Thomasin answered, 'You must not be surprised, Your Grace, if she has little to say to you, if she is overawed. We have lived our lives among plain people.'

And I thought, 'Thomasin hates her; and yet she has been only kind to us . . .'

Thomasin thought she had seen the last of the Duchess, with her plain-speaking. But she was wrong. The weather continued bad, and we had no visitors for three days. And no letters; but we did not look for any while the north winds would be making the passage to the lighthouse dangerous. And I woke from a troubled daylight sleep to see a woman enter the room. I did not at first know her, I thought it was Mrs Shields. But when I looked longer I saw it was the Duchess in a plain grey gown, and alone. She looked around for a chair, I thought, and not finding one she knelt at my bedside, and took my hand. She stayed a little while in silence – or what silence the room offered, for it was full of a painful sound – someone somewhere fighting to draw every breath.

Then she said she had made calves'-foot jelly with her own hands, and brought it in case I might be able to digest it. And she put a hand upon my forehead, and smoothed back my hair, and asked if I would speak for her, and for her good Hugh, before the throne of heaven.

And I summoned strength to say I could not undertake it, because I feared I should go to hell for the sin of avarice.

'Oh, no, dear Grace!' she said. 'You have not desired the gifts the world has given you! And only yesterday the Archdeacon told me he regarded you most highly as a beautiful example of lowly virtue! Be assured, if the world closes to you, it is heaven that shall open.'

I felt a sort of sorrow for her, that she should kneel at my pillow and request my prayers, and a rueful respect for my sister, whose sharp tongue had made so great a lady wear a humble dress; but we were troubled no more by the Duchess, or by Doctor Barnfather, for Mr Shields's letter to Father had reached him at last at Longstone through the autumn storms, and he had come in haste to take me home to Balmboro', to be among my own people.

· 23 ·

Once he got us to Balmboro' – he had borrowed a cart and horse to convey us – Father put me in an armchair by the fire. I had withstood the journey better than he had feared I might, but the truth is I was uplifted by joy at being almost home, and a little dejected only when I understood he would not take me all the way to Longstone.

'What?' he said, 'in an open boat?' He was so angry with Thomasin, because she had not truthfully written how ill I was, that he could scarce speak to her, and I thought him unfair, and told him with what force I could, but words came with difficulty to me, how well she had cared for me.

Within an hour or so of our being within, Father sat down to write to the Duke, to tell him that he had removed me, and Thomasin would keep Dr Barnfather furnished with particulars. And then he went off to the islands, leaving a kiss upon my forehead, and with a most sad face.

That was some days since. I am surrounded with kindness. An acquaintance at Wooler has written imploring me to drink asses' milk; Mr Smeddle has brought some more inscribed parchments, and medals. The parson has come in to pray with me.

Many of my friends from long ago come by. Mr Shields has written me a long letter about spiritual matters, and the good of my soul, and asks me not to let anyone hinder me from reading and thinking and making preparation to meet my God. And there have been three times messengers from the Duke. He answered my father, not pleased, I think, but not taking offence at my being brought here, and there have been two visits from his lawyers with talk of the trusts, and the funds, and papers and a will for me to sign. I have steadfastly refused to sign papers, or talk of money. I asked the second lawyer – he came with Mr Smeddle, hoping to use his influence – what would become of the money, if I made no will.

They glanced at one another, and the lawyer answered, 'All will accrue to your mother and father, as your next-of-kin.'

'Very well, then,' I said. 'Father has strength enough to bear it.'

The lawyer said, 'Smeddle, we are too late, I fancy. Her mind is unclear; she cannot make a binding will.'

Thomasin shushed them, and bustled them out, and let me rest. But I could not avoid knowing that they all thought I was dying. So I made my own kind of will. I called Thomasin, and she sat with me with a pencil and wrote down my gifts. My gold watch to her, for all her loving kindness to me in my need; my gold medal to brother William, the other medals one each to Robert and Brooks and George, the silk mantle to Jane, the silver cestus to

Betsy, and so on, till everyone had something to remember me by. Thomasin was weeping like a silly baby all this while, but I felt as though I were putting off a heavy garment, and moving free.

'Gracie, there is something else,' she said. 'Mr John Reay is outside. He has ridden hard from Durham, where he heard news of your being ill. He is waiting in the church. Will you see him? Shall I bring him to you?'

'No,' I said.

'But Gracie, he will be much distressed. He tells me that you summoned him – that his approach is permitted. Is is not true?'

'Why came he not sooner? He is too late.'

'He says your letter followed him and missed him on his journeys for some time. And that he would have come by and by, only that he did not know until just now that you are ill.'

'Did it need my illness to bring him? He is too late.'

'But you did allow him – you did accept him as a follower?'

'He may follow me anywhere I may now go!' I said. 'But I don't want to see him.'

'I will tell him so,' she said.

It was a fine autumn day, of soft sunlight, and too warm within the room. I struggled from the close bed to the chair, and looked out of the window to the sunlit grasses, parched pale gold by the summer's heat, that rippled in the sea airs between the grave-stones. I watched people come and go in the quiet street, the light of the sky, the growing grasses, the scrap of blue sea that showed above the graveyard wall. I did not wish to look at any of it. I remembered the wide sweep of the moving water at Longstone, at a calm high tide. I remembered how on quiet nights the moon and stars were doubled in the shining waters and in the sky above, the sky and waters seamless in the darkness. I remembered the little bright dancing whitecaps among the rocks in summer, and the uplifted flight of the gliding seabirds. And I thought, I am not dying, just burdened and sad. If only I could free my mind of fears about the money, I would be better right away! I could go home then. I have been a prey to nightmare; but I am sure the truth is not so terrible. I must just remember what I was thinking about that morning, and all will be well.

I tried to remember, and I could not. After supper I slept. I was sleeping covered with many blankets, in the chair beside the fire, for sitting upright I coughed less. And the nightmare came over me the most terrible I have ever had it. I was washing blood from the money, and putting it in piles to be given to Father and Mother. It would not come clean. It defiled my grasping fingers so that I looked at my hands in loathing – I cried out, and woke. Thomasin was sleeping peacefully on her mattress on the floor. She slept there to be near me if I needed anything, but she had not woken now.

I thought, 'If I could just glimpse the Fernes again, I would surely remember clearly. It is so long since I was home; I need to see . . .' I took my cloak from the hook behind the door, and quietly slid the bolt, and stepped out. It was a cold night, and the stars were blanked out by a fierce scudding sky. I pulled the cloak round me, and went with what haste I could down the silent street. The great bulk of the castle stood in darker outline against the night at the foot of the street, with only one light showing in a high window where one of the Crewe Trust servants worked late. It was a struggle to me to ascend the castle mound; my legs were shaky. I had been too much abed. So I went round, into the grass-tufted towans below the castle cliff. At once a great wind struck me from off the sea, and with it came a sudden cold shower of heavy rain. The sandy slopes slipped under my feet, and I fought to get high enough to have a lookout towards home. I could feel the bitter cold air burn a pathway through my lungs at every breath; I thought it would scour me clean.

I was engulfed in waves of sand, and wet to the skin in the downpour, and at last I found my way to the underhang of the castle cliff, just high enough to see out to sea, and find in the gloom the tiny spark of the Longstone light through the storm. I leaned against the rough rock and supposed myself again in such a tempest, and with a boat to launch and go . . .

'Miss Darling? Grace Darling!' Someone was shouting at me. 'God in Heaven, what do you here?'

I opened my eyes with difficulty. Someone grasped me, and I slumped down. 'You are ill! You are wet! What do you here?'

I found myself lifted to my feet by Mr Tulloch.

'My poor girl, you are wet through! What possesses you to walk here at dead of night?'

'You do so too,' I said. 'It is as mad for you as for me.'

'You are right,' he said. 'I cannot tear myself away. I cannot cease to relive, to remember what happened out there. Your good deed . . .'

'Ah, but it was not a good deed,' I said. 'Has nobody told you? There was money at stake. That's why I did it!'

I thought he would shrink from me in loathing, call me cormorant. He seized me roughly, and shook me in a fury. 'It doesn't matter!' he cried. 'It doesn't matter a groat why you did it! If you did it for rage and spite and greed, am I the less living for that? Or are the others less safe and dry? Are you raving?'

A strange sort of lightness was coming over me. It didn't matter! He went on, 'What coin was ever minted, Miss Darling, that made a brave man of a coward, or could buy what you did for me?'

He put an arm round me then, saying, 'Let me help you.' I could scarcely go, though I felt as light as a leaf. He struggled to bring me back through the sandy tracks round the castle and into the town. At least when we had the castle at our backs we were in the lee of the wind. There we saw a wavering light going; someone walking with a lantern. Mr Tulloch called loudly for help. Thomas Cuthbertson came to us with the light. He was going to his mother's house, I supposed. He held the light up, and saw.

'Can you take her other arm, and help us home?' said Mr Tulloch. 'I found her wandering.'

Thomas put down the lantern, and picked me up bodily, and strode up the street with me. I felt his strength, his firm grasp. He had me home swiftly, Mr Tulloch coming after with the lantern, and they hammered upon the door. Thomasin opened in alarm, and Thomas strode in, and put me down in the chair. The water ran from my garments upon the floor. The rain flowed on Thomas's cheeks, I saw it as he set me down.

'There's no weight to yow, Gracie. Yow's gone like the snow,' he said huskily. Then he had gone, to run round wakening the neighbours, fetching women to help Thomasin. They made me a bath of hot water, they rubbed at my freezing limbs. 'How had she the strength to do it?' wailed Thomasin.

'I told you I was better!' I said to her.

'Oh, Grace, what a wicked thing to do!' she cried, but I had Mr Tulloch's words ringing in my mind, and was full of joy.

I think I slept for some days. When I woke, Father was in the room, and Mother. Mother must have feared for me greatly to bestir herself to come, and I smiled at her mistake. I was full of wonder at myself. How could I have so far forgotten myself, how could I have been so put about as not to see that *it didn't matter*! It didn't make a ha'porth of difference *why*! And I felt light as air. I felt as though my body had long been a burden to my soul, and was suddenly lighter far to carry. I thought I could have danced with lightness, like the leaves on the wind outside.

I coughed suddenly, and a great gout of blood spilled from me upon the bed-cover.

'Look!' I said to Thomasin. 'That is what I have been trying to cough up all these days. It is out now, and my breath is clear!' And why does the silly girl look so glum? I wondered.

There is light of uncommon beauty shining in the window. I did not know the beam would reach so far away; I did not know how beautiful the Long-stone light would look to someone drifting in dark waters, and I wish to see it better. I say, 'Father, lift me up . . .'

· Author's Note ·

Grace Darling died of consumption in her father's arms in the cottage at Balmboro' in which she had been born, on 20th October, 1842. Unlike many heroines and heroes, Grace Darling really did the brave deed for which she is famous, without any shadow of a doubt. This is a novel, and I have imagined the thoughts and words of the characters, but otherwise the first part of this book tells the story of the shipwreck and rescue as exactly and truthfully as I can.

The second part is much more free, but gives a broadly truthful impression of the remaining years of Grace's short life. All the letters quoted in the book (except for that on page 163) are real, and all extracts are verbatim. It is known that one of the artists who came to paint her fell in love with her, and it is known that a young man walked in her family party at her funeral. We do not know who these people were, and my version is imaginary.

There are two important books about Grace Darling. The first is an encyclopaedic biography by Constance Smedley, *Grace Darling and Her Times* (1932), on which all subsequent work relies. The second is *Grace Darling, Maid and Myth* by Richard

Armstrong (1965), which first addressed the problem of the bad odour in which Grace was held at North Sunderland. The 150th anniversary of the deed saw an excellent short book for young children by Helen Cresswell, *The Story of Grace Darling* (1988), and a lavishly illustrated volume by Jessica Mitford, *Grace Had an English Heart* (1988), in which the hysterical 'hype' which surrounded Grace Darling is vividly and amusingly displayed.

It has always been part of Grace's story, and a mystery, why, from that day to this, she aroused resentment instead of admiration among the people of North Sunderland, now called Seahouses; perhaps today, when much more recent public subscriptions in the aftermath of disasters have caused resentment among those closely concerned, we might find some charitable understanding for this situation.

The resentment has extended to Richard Armstrong's *Grace Darling, Maid and Myth*, which put forward a theory, based probably on his local knowledge, but not citing written evidence, that everyone's behaviour could best be understood as a competition for the bounties which were regularly paid for rescues. In spite of the scorn heaped on this book it is certainly true that bounties were paid, and people expected them when they set out on rescue missions. My daughter read for me in the Archives of the Crewe Trustees, deposited in the County Library at Newcastle; and in their account books, and in numerous newspaper reports of shipwreck, she found very sufficient evidence for everything Richard Armstrong has to say on the matter.

The public at large always believed Grace Darling acted disinterestedly. The idea that a young woman had risked her life for others without any hope of reward was a strong inspirational force in the development of the Royal National Lifeboat Institution. Lifeboatmen today set out at need into terrible dangers, for negligible reward, and their courage is beyond praise.

I agree very strongly with Richard Armstrong that no money has ever been minted which could pay for such conduct.

· *Acknowledgement* ·

I have had generous help from my daughter, Margaret Paton Walsh, and from Derek Calderwood, Esq., Hon Curator of the Grace Darling Museum, Bamburgh, and much encouragement from Bruce Hunter and from Maurice Lyon. Marni Hodgkin and Belinda Hollyer read the MS for me, and I would also like to thank Aran John, then of Kestrel, who first proposed the subject to me. I also thank John Rowe Townsend for unfailing and generous encouragement, and help in everything to do with the book, great and small.